Disney Tangled The Series

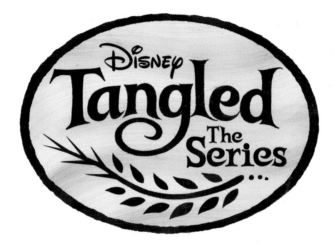

Facebook: **facebook.com/idwpublishing**
Twitter: **@idwpublishing**
YouTube: **youtube.com/idwpublishing**
Tumblr: **tumblr.idwpublishing.com**
Instagram: **instagram.com/idwpublishing**

ISBN: 978-1-68405-198-4   21 20 19 18   3 4 5 6

COVER
DIOGO SAITO

Cover Colors
VITA EFREMOVA
& EKATERINA MYSHALOVA

EDITOR
SARAH GAYDOS

COLLECTION EDITORS
JUSTIN EISINGER
and ALONZO SIMON

COLLECTION DESIGNER
CLYDE GRAPA

PUBLISHER
TED ADAMS

Ted Adams, CEO & Publisher
Greg Goldstein, President & COO
Robbie Robbins, EVP/Sr. Graphic Artist
Chris Ryall, Chief Creative Officer
David Hedgecock, Editor-in-Chief
Laurie Windrow, Senior VP of Sales & Marketing
Matthew Ruzicka, CPA, Chief Financial Officer
Lorelei Bunjes, VP of Digital Services
Jerry Bennington, VP of New Product Development

Special thanks to Eugene Paraszczuk, Julie Dorris, Manny Mederos, Roberto Santillo, Camilla Vedove, Stefano Ambrosio, Chris Troise, and Carlotta Quattrocolo.

Before Ever After

Adapted by: Alessandro Ferrari
Layouts: Ivan Shavrin
Cleanups: Rosa La Barbera
& Monica Catalano
Paints: Ludmila Steblianko,
Alesya Baarsukova,
Vita Efremova,
& Anna Beliashova
Letters: Chris Dickey

Hair Today

Writer: Scott Peterson
Layouts: Diogo Saito
Cleanup/Ink: Rosa La Barbera
Colors: Vita Efremova
& Ekaterina Myshalova
Letters: Chris Dickey

Princess Cassandra

Writer: Scott Peterson
Layouts: Diogo Saito
Cleanup/Ink: Rosa La Barbera
Colors: Vita Efremova
& Ekaterina Myshalova
Letters: Chris Dickey

Greetings

Writer: Scott Peterson
Layouts: Diogo Saito
Cleanup/Ink: Rosa La Barbera
Colors: Vita Efremova
& Ekaterina Myshalova
Letters: Chris Dickey

The Perfect Joke

Writer: Alessandro Ferrari
Layouts: Roberto Di Salvo
Cleanup/Ink: Rosa La Barbera
Colors: Vita Efremova
& Ekaterina Myshalova
Letters: Chris Dickey

A Hero's Reputation

Writer: Scott Peterson
Layouts: Ivan Shavrin
Cleanups: Rosa La Barbera
& Monica Catalano
Paints: Ludmila Steblianko,
Alesya Baarsukova,
Vita Efremova,
& Anna Beliashova
Letters: Chris Dickey

Caution: Wet Hair

Writer: Scott Peterson
Layouts: Diogo Saito
Cleanup/Ink: Rosa La Barbera
Colors: Vita Efremova
& Ekaterina Myshalova
Letters: Chris Dickey

Lost

Writer: Scott Peterson
Layouts: Diogo Saito
Cleanup/Ink: Rosa La Barbera
Colors: Vita Efremova
& Ekaterina Myshalova
Letters: Chris Dickey

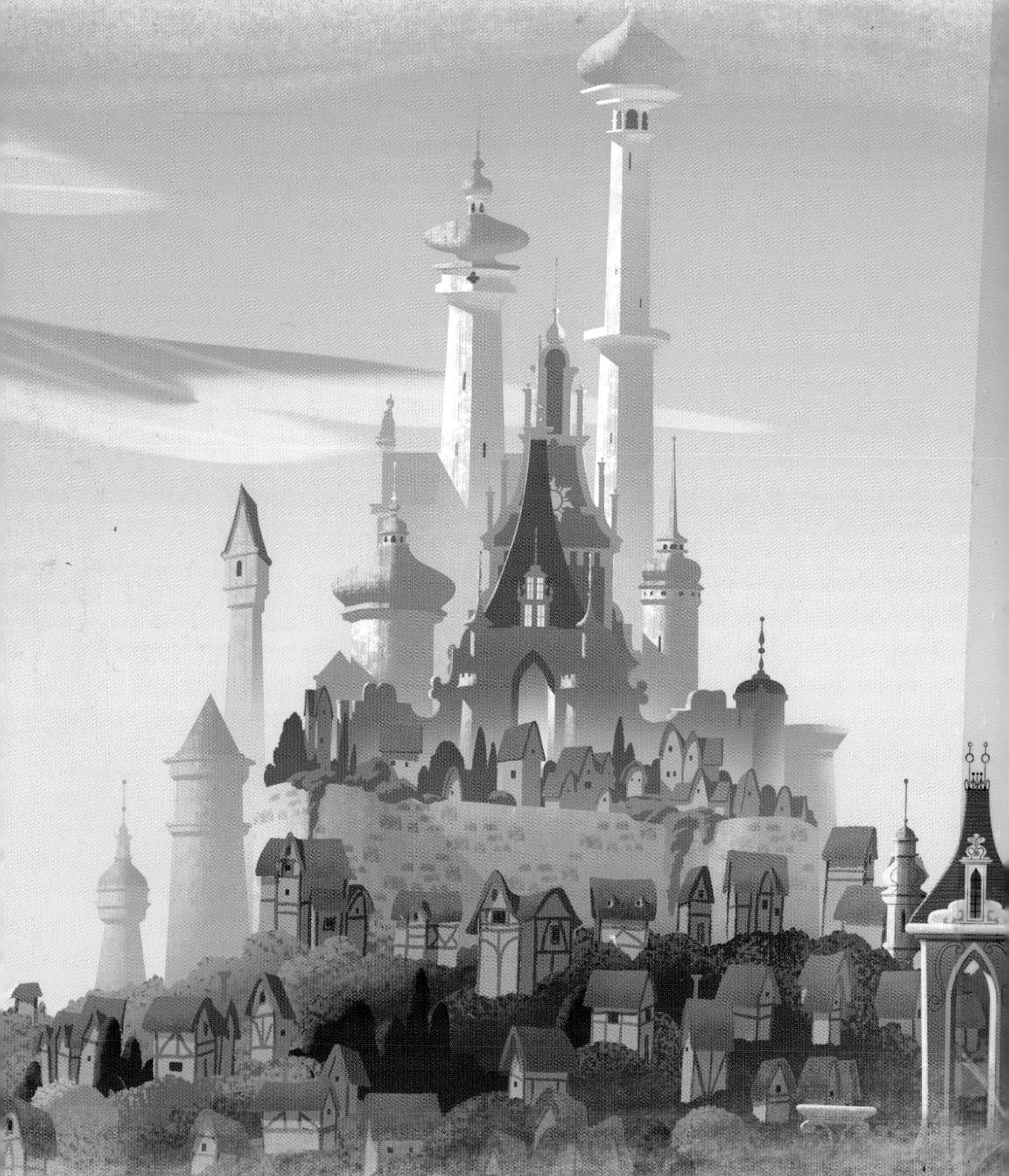

Before Ever After

Adapted by: Alessandro Ferrari
Layouts: Ivan Shavrin
Cleanups: Rosa La Barbera
    & Monica Catalano
Paints: Ludmila Steblianko,
    Alesya Baarsukova,
    Vita Efremova,
    & Anna Beliashova
Letters: Chris Dickey

Hair Today

Writer: Scott Peterson
Layouts: Diogo Saito
Cleanup/Ink: Rosa La Barbera
Colors: Vita Efremova
    & Ekaterina Myshalova
Letters: Chris Dickey

Princess Cassandra

Writer: Scott Peterson
Layouts: Diogo Saito
Cleanup/Ink: Rosa La Barbera
Colors: Vita Efremova
    & Ekaterina Myshalova
Letters: Chris Dickey

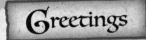

Greetings

Writer: Scott Peterson
Layouts: Diogo Saito
Cleanup/Ink: Rosa La Barbera
Colors: Vita Efremova
    & Ekaterina Myshalova
Letters: Chris Dickey

The Perfect Joke

Writer: Alessandro Ferrari
Layouts: Roberto Di Salvo
Cleanup/Ink: Rosa La Barbera
Colors: Vita Efremova
    & Ekaterina Myshalova
Letters: Chris Dickey

A Hero's Reputation

Writer: Scott Peterson
Layouts: Ivan Shavrin
Cleanups: Rosa La Barbera
    & Monica Catalano
Paints: Ludmila Steblianko,
    Alesya Baarsukova,
    Vita Efremova,
    & Anna Beliashova
Letters: Chris Dickey

Caution: Wet Hair

Writer: Scott Peterson
Layouts: Diogo Saito
Cleanup/Ink: Rosa La Barbera
Colors: Vita Efremova
    & Ekaterina Myshalova
Letters: Chris Dickey

Lost

Writer: Scott Peterson
Layouts: Diogo Saito
Cleanup/Ink: Rosa La Barbera
Colors: Vita Efremova
    & Ekaterina Myshalova
Letters: Chris Dickey

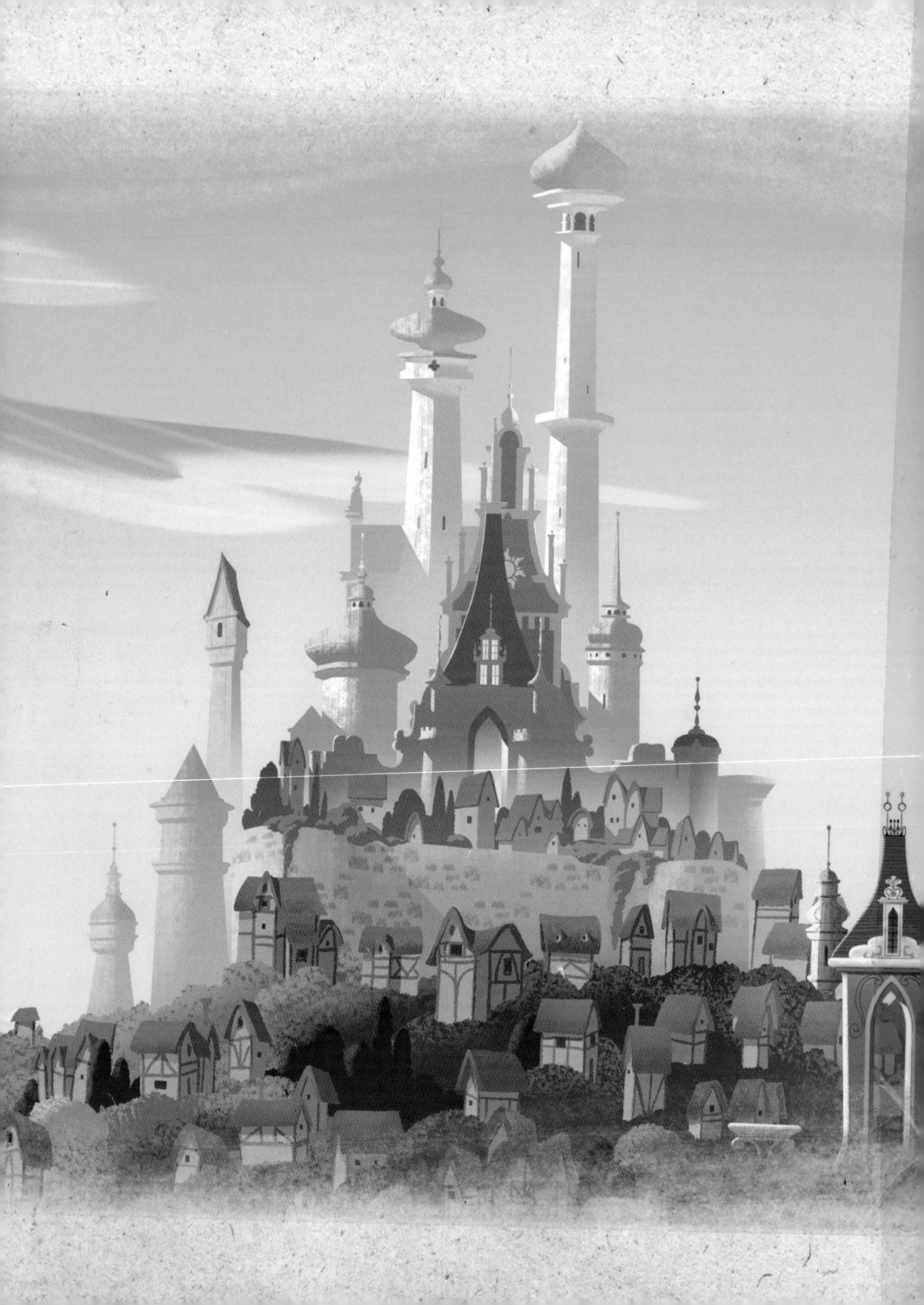

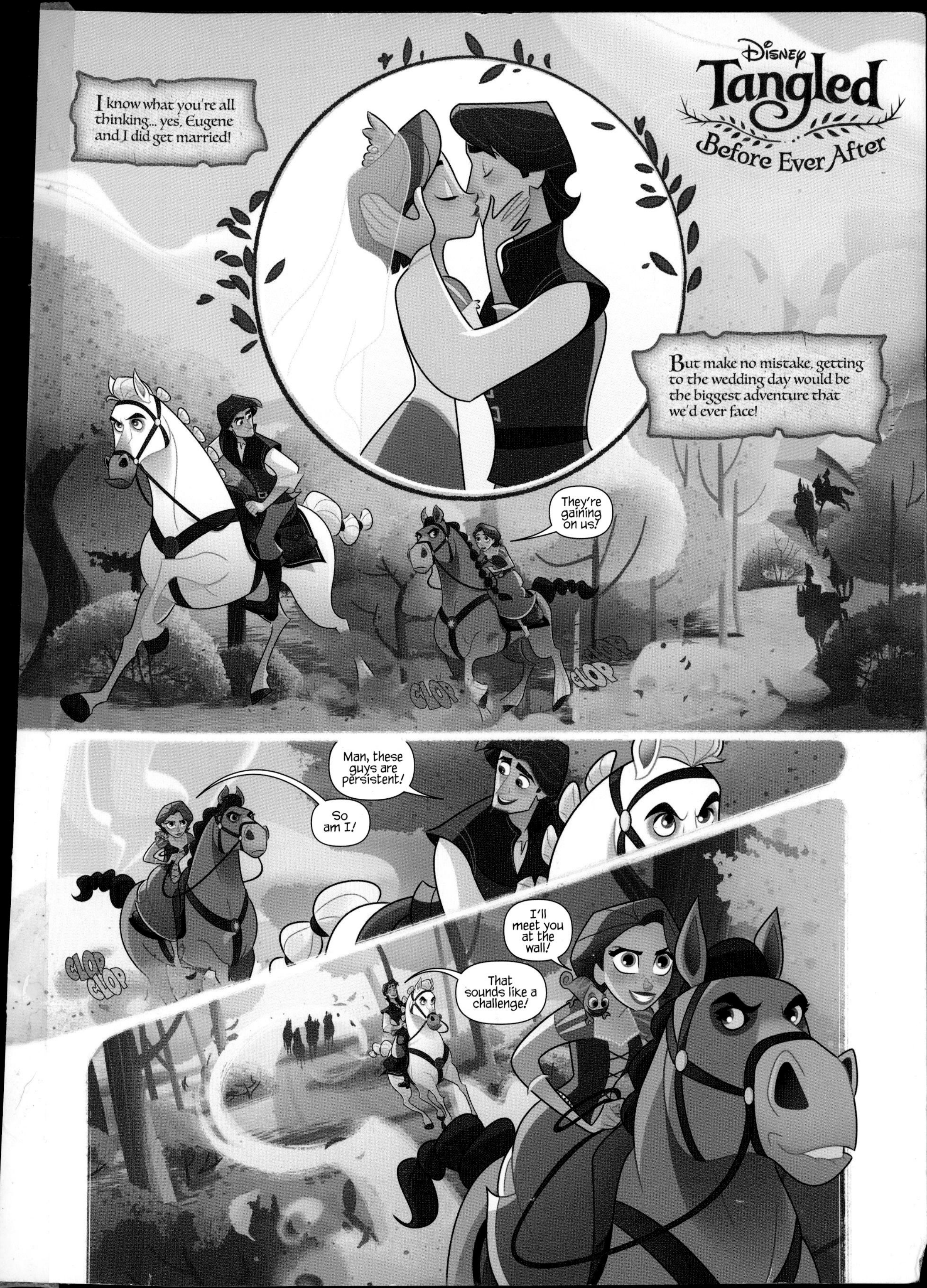
Disney
Tangled
Before Ever After
I know what you're all thinking... yes, Eugene and I did get married!
But make no mistake, getting to the wedding day would be the biggest adventure that we'd ever face!
They're gaining on us!
CLOP
CLOP CLOP
Man, these guys are persistent!
So am I!
CLOP CLOP
I'll meet you at the wall!
That sounds like a challenge!

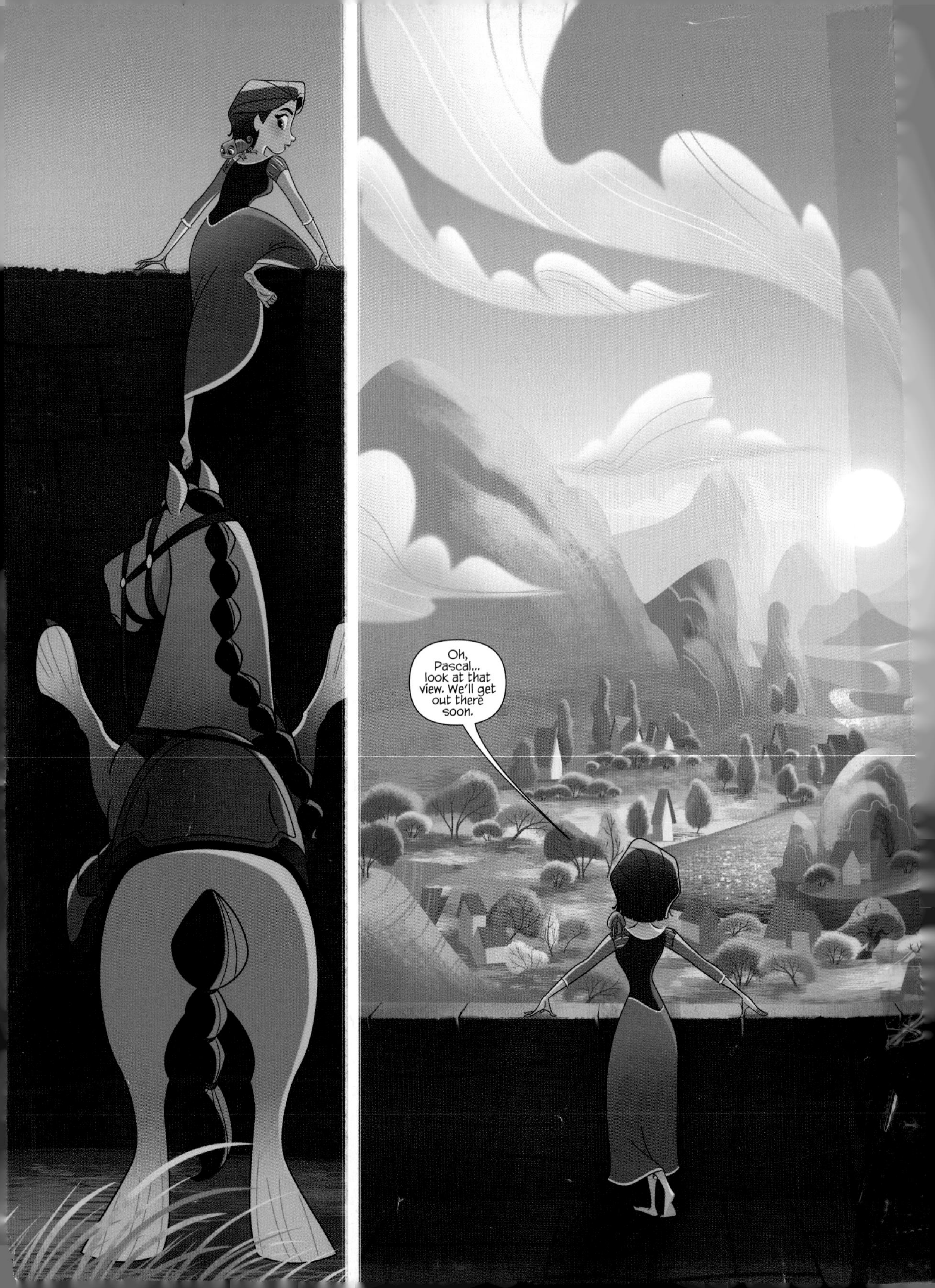
Oh, Pascal... look at that view. We'll get out there soon.

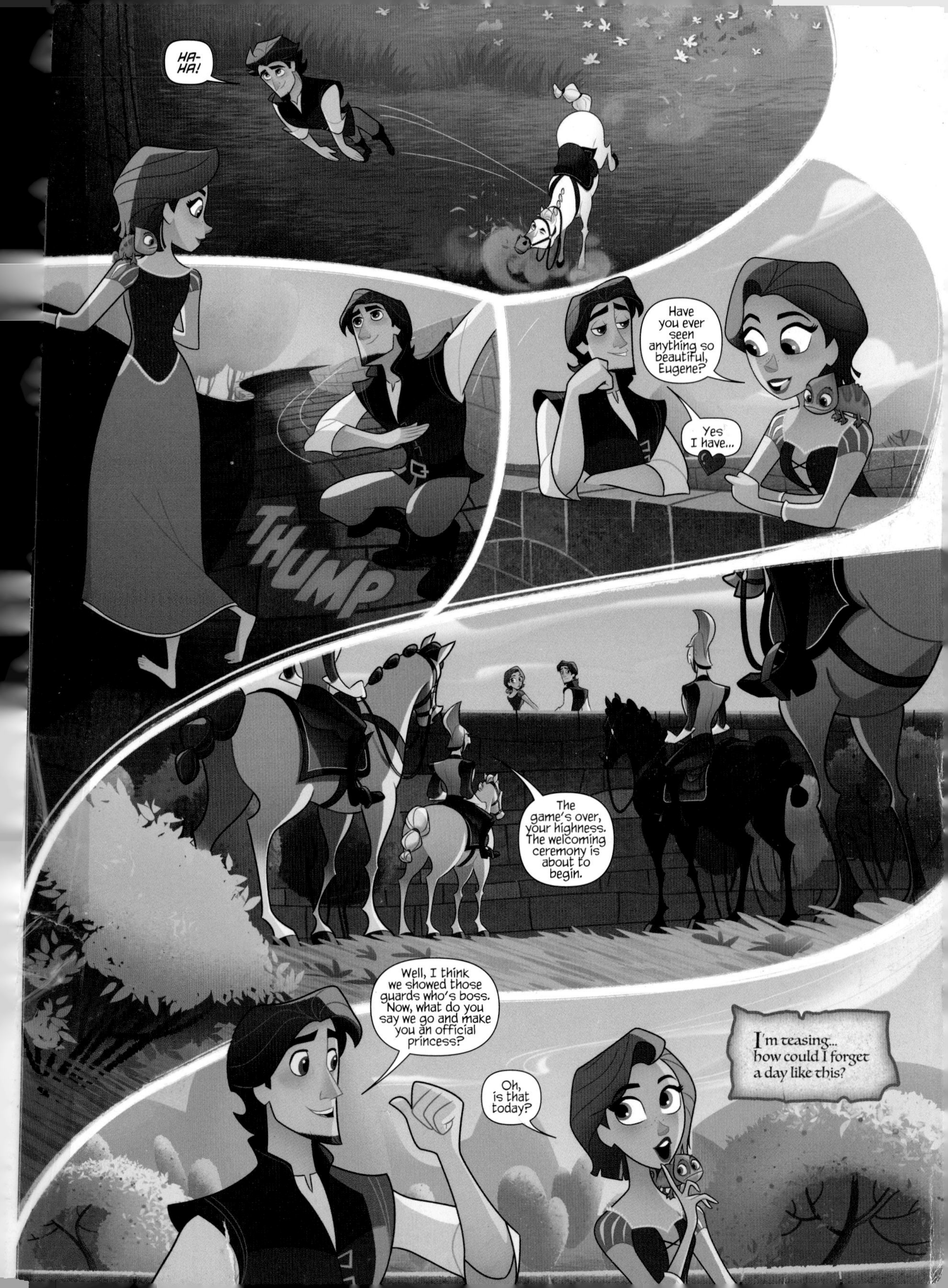
HA-HA!
THUMP
Have you ever seen anything so beautiful, Eugene?
Yes I have...
The game's over, your highness. The welcoming ceremony is about to begin.
Well, I think we showed those guards who's boss. Now, what do you say we go and make you an official princess?
Oh, is that today?
I'm teasing... how could I forget a day like this?

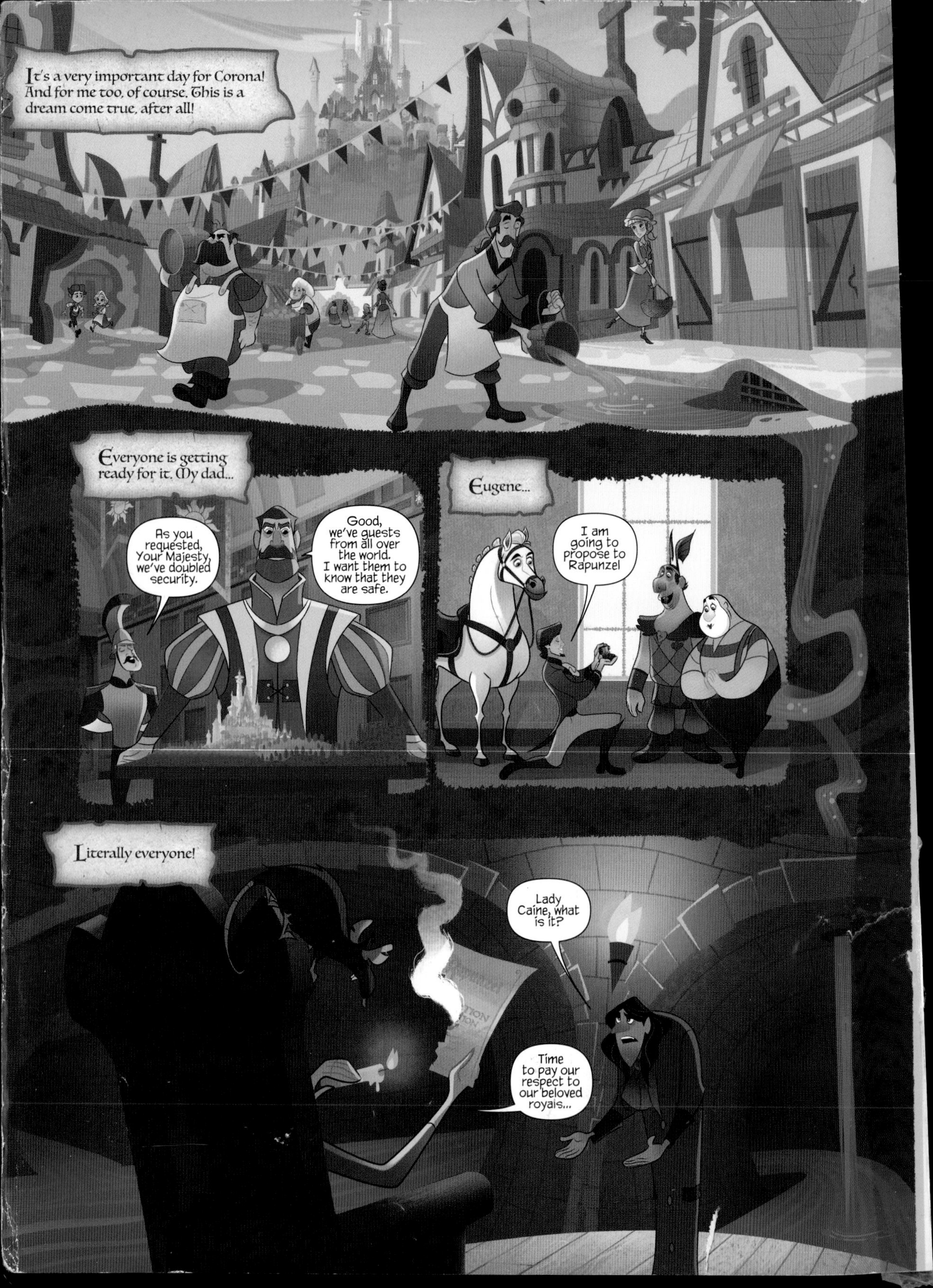
It's a very important day for Corona! And for me too, of course. This is a dream come true, after all!
Everyone is getting ready for it. My dad...
As you requested, Your Majesty, we've doubled security.
Good, we've guests from all over the world. I want them to know that they are safe.
Eugene...
I am going to propose to Rapunzel
Literally everyone!
Lady Caine, what is it?
Time to pay our respect to our beloved royals...

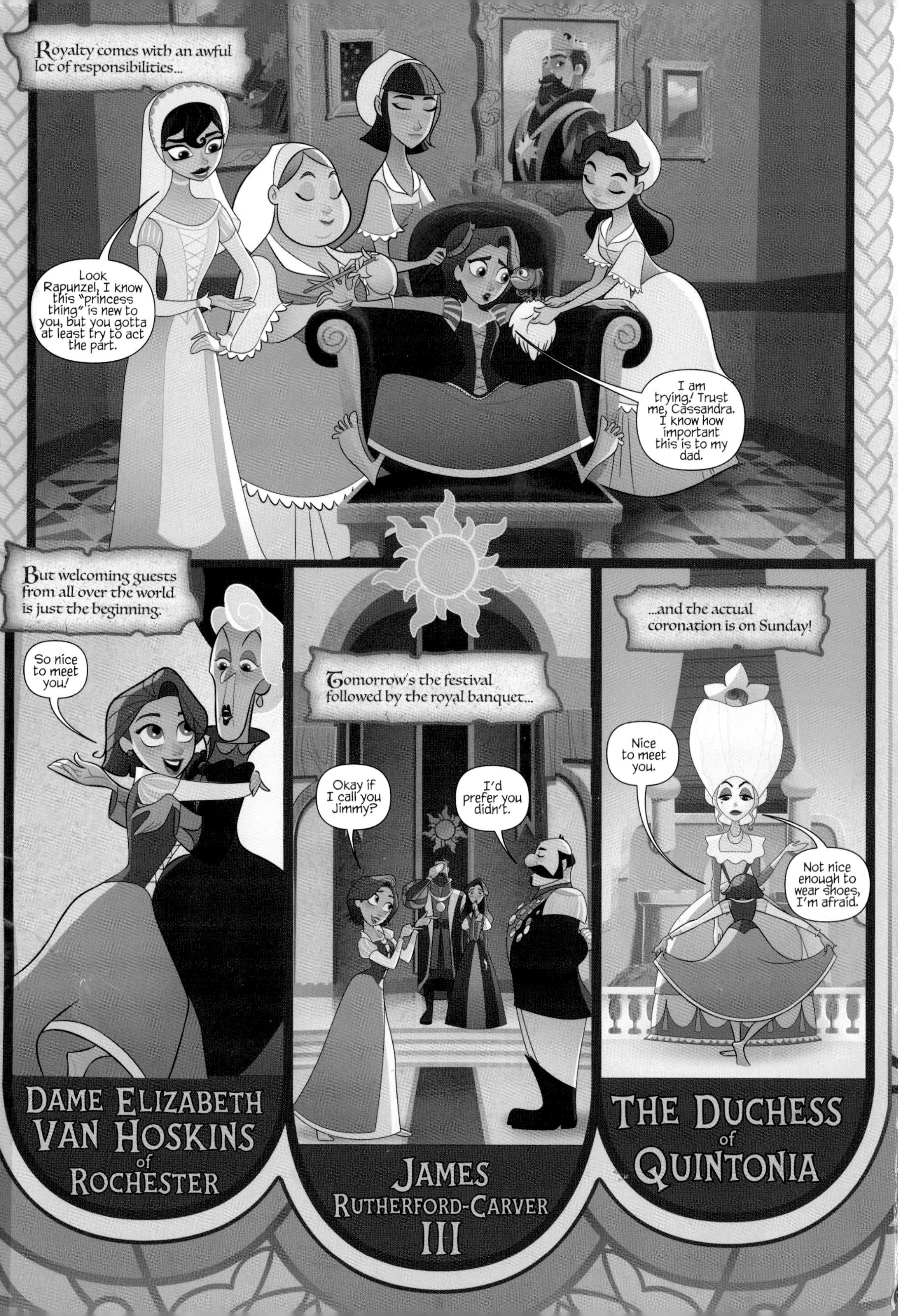
Royalty comes with an awful lot of responsibilities...
Look Rapunzel, I know this "princess thing" is new to you, but you gotta at least try to act the part.
I am trying! Trust me, Cassandra. I know how important this is to my dad.
But welcoming guests from all over the world is just the beginning.
So nice to meet you!
DAME ELIZABETH VAN HOSKINS of ROCHESTER
Tomorrow's the festival followed by the royal banquet...
Okay if I call you Jimmy?
I'd prefer you didn't.
JAMES RUTHERFORD-CARVER III
...and the actual coronation is on Sunday!
Nice to meet you.
Not nice enough to wear shoes, I'm afraid.
THE DUCHESS of QUINTONIA

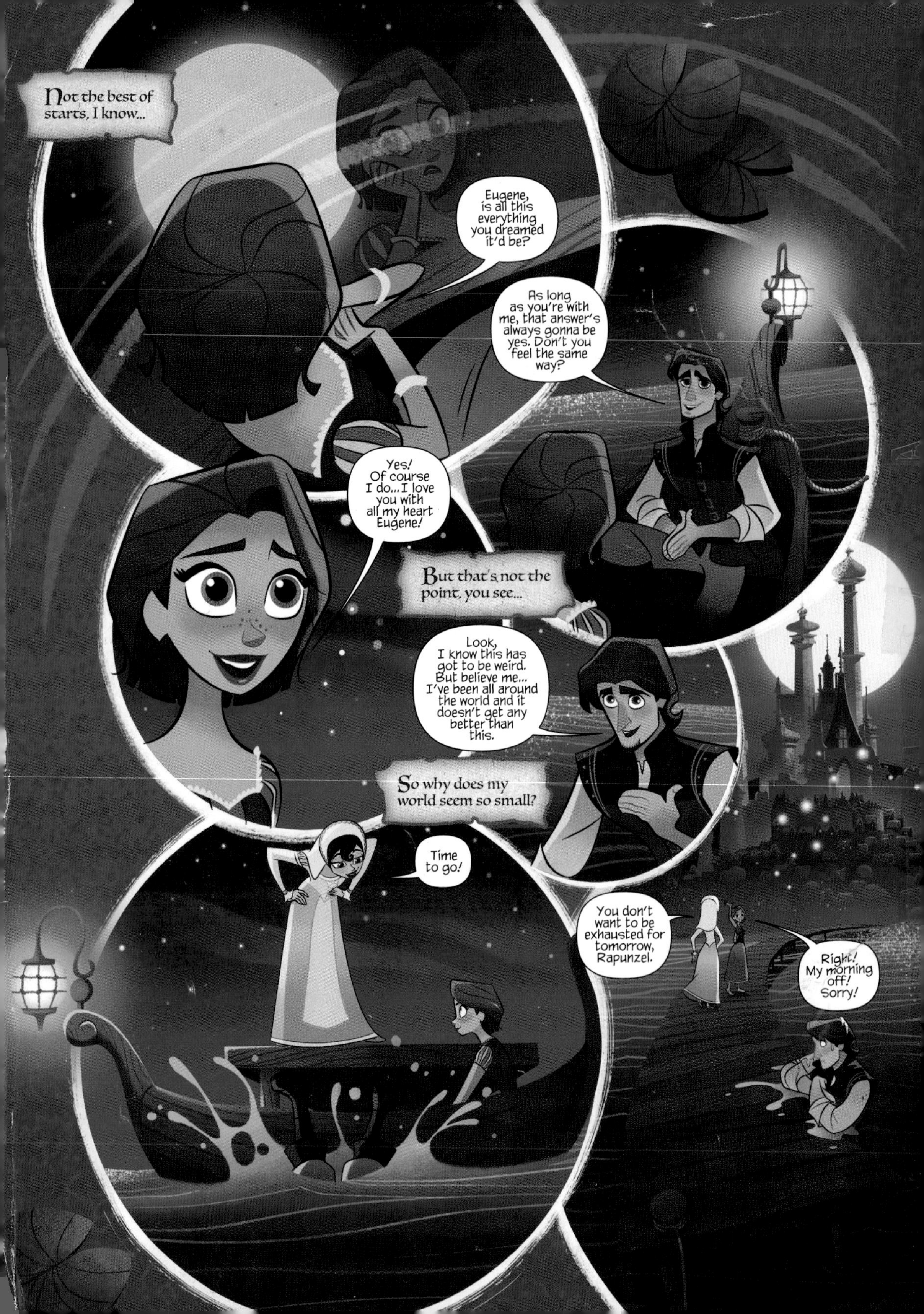

Not the best of starts, I know...
Eugene, is all this everything you dreamed it'd be?
As long as you're with me, that answer's always gonna be yes. Don't you feel the same way?
Yes! Of course I do... I love you with all my heart Eugene!
But that's not the point, you see...
Look, I know this has got to be weird. But believe me... I've been all around the world and it doesn't get any better than this.
So why does my world seem so small?
Time to go!
You don't want to be exhausted for tomorrow, Rapunzel.
Right! My morning off! Sorry!

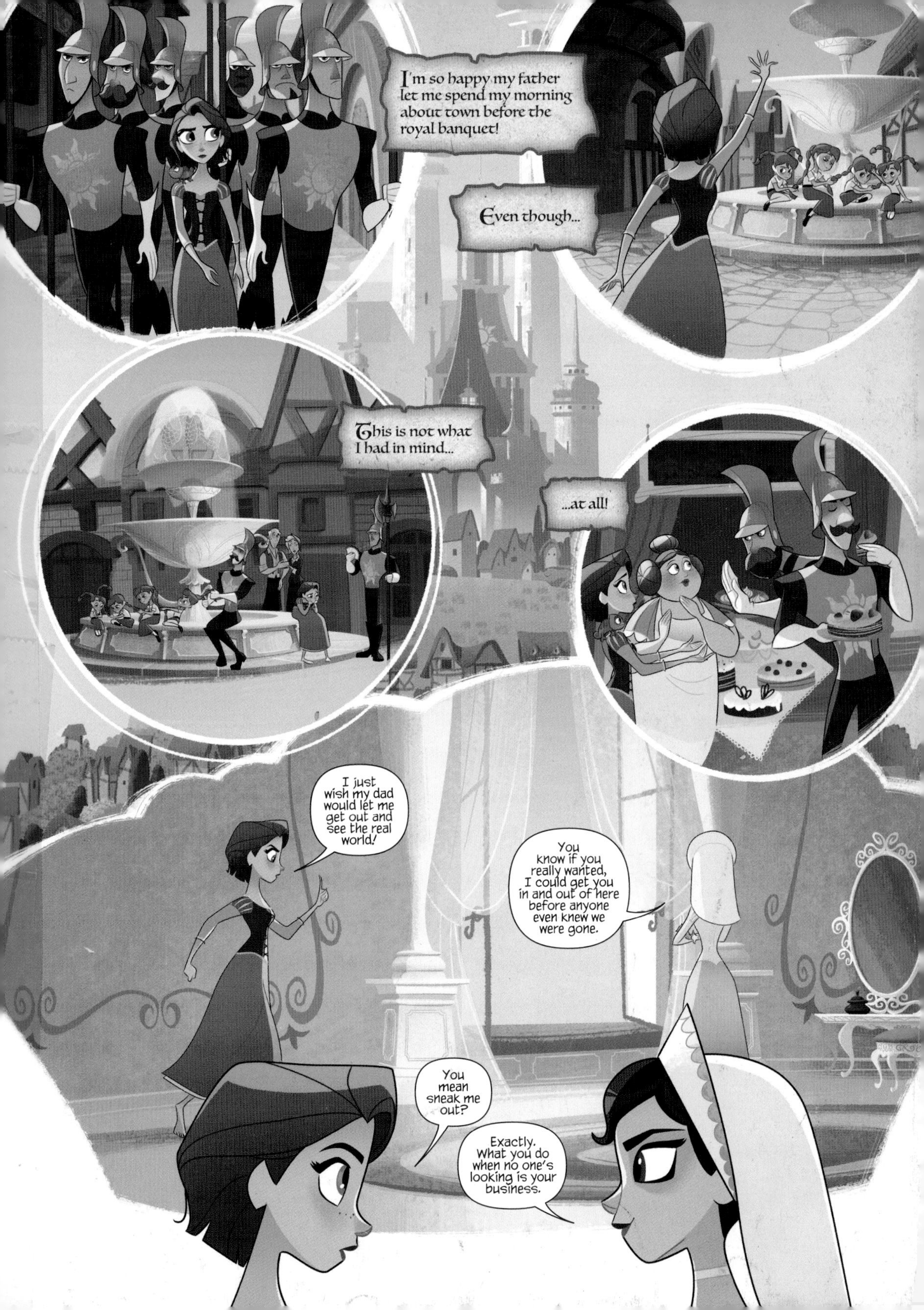
I'm so happy my father let me spend my morning about town before the royal banquet!
Even though...
This is not what I had in mind...
...at all!
I just wish my dad would let me get out and see the real world!
You know if you really wanted, I could get you in and out of here before anyone even knew we were gone.
You mean sneak me out?
Exactly. What you do when no one's looking is your business.

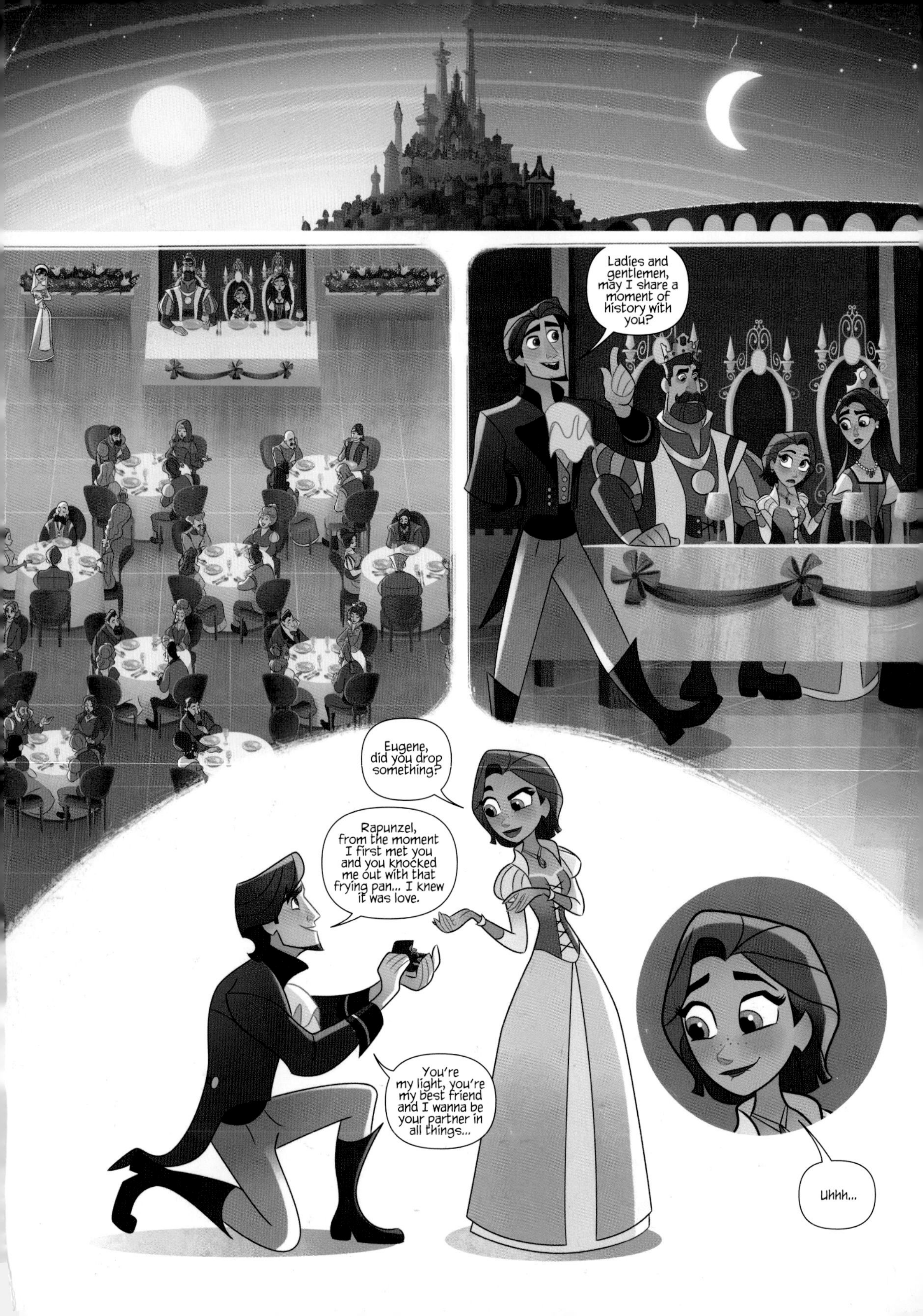
Ladies and gentlemen, may I share a moment of history with you?
Eugene, did you drop something?
Rapunzel, from the moment I first met you and you knocked me out with that frying pan... I knew it was love.
You're my light, you're my best friend and I wanna be your partner in all things...
Uhhh...

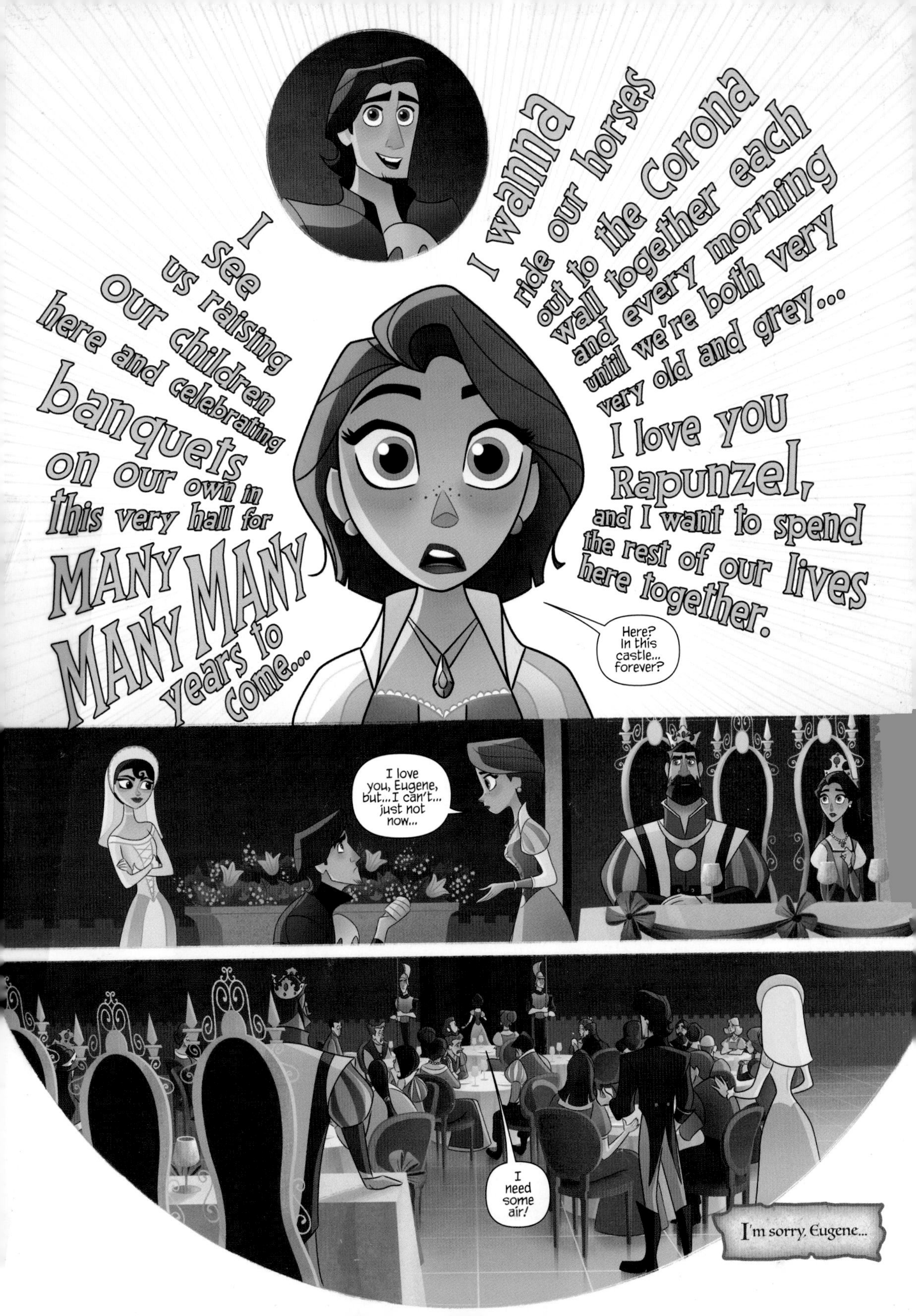
I see us raising our children here and celebrating banquets on our own in this very hall for MANY MANY MANY MANY years to come...
I wanna ride our horses out to the Corona wall together each and every morning until we're both very very old and grey...
I love YOU Rapunzel, and I want to spend the rest of our lives here together.
Here? In this castle... forever?
I love you, Eugene, but... I can't... just not now...
I need some air!
I'm sorry, Eugene...

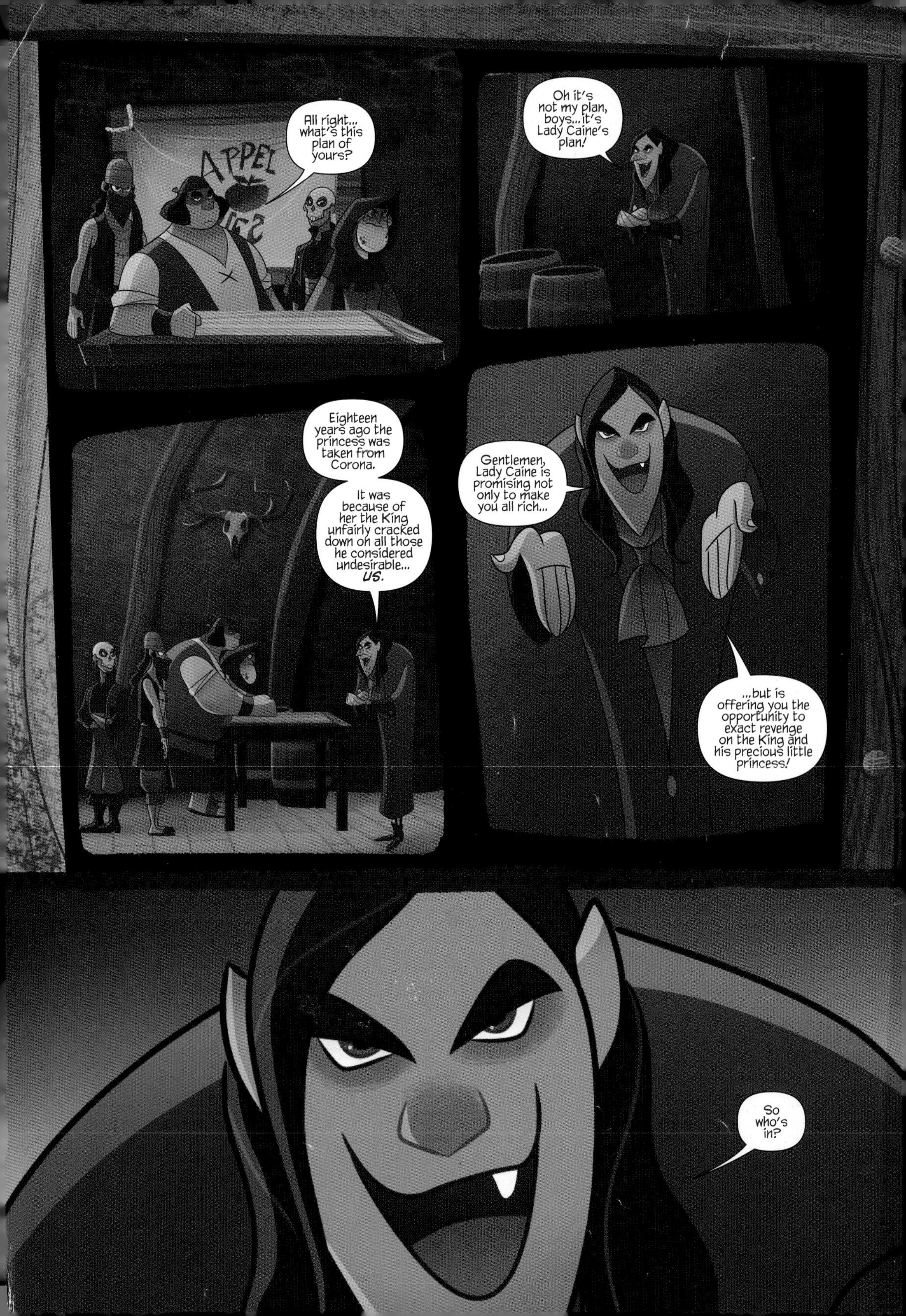
All right... what's this plan of yours?
Oh it's not my plan, boys... it's Lady Caine's plan!
Eighteen years ago the princess was taken from Corona.
It was because of her the King unfairly cracked down on all those he considered undesirable... US.
Gentlemen, Lady Caine is promising not only to make you all rich...
...but is offering you the opportunity to exact revenge on the King and his precious little princess!
So who's in?

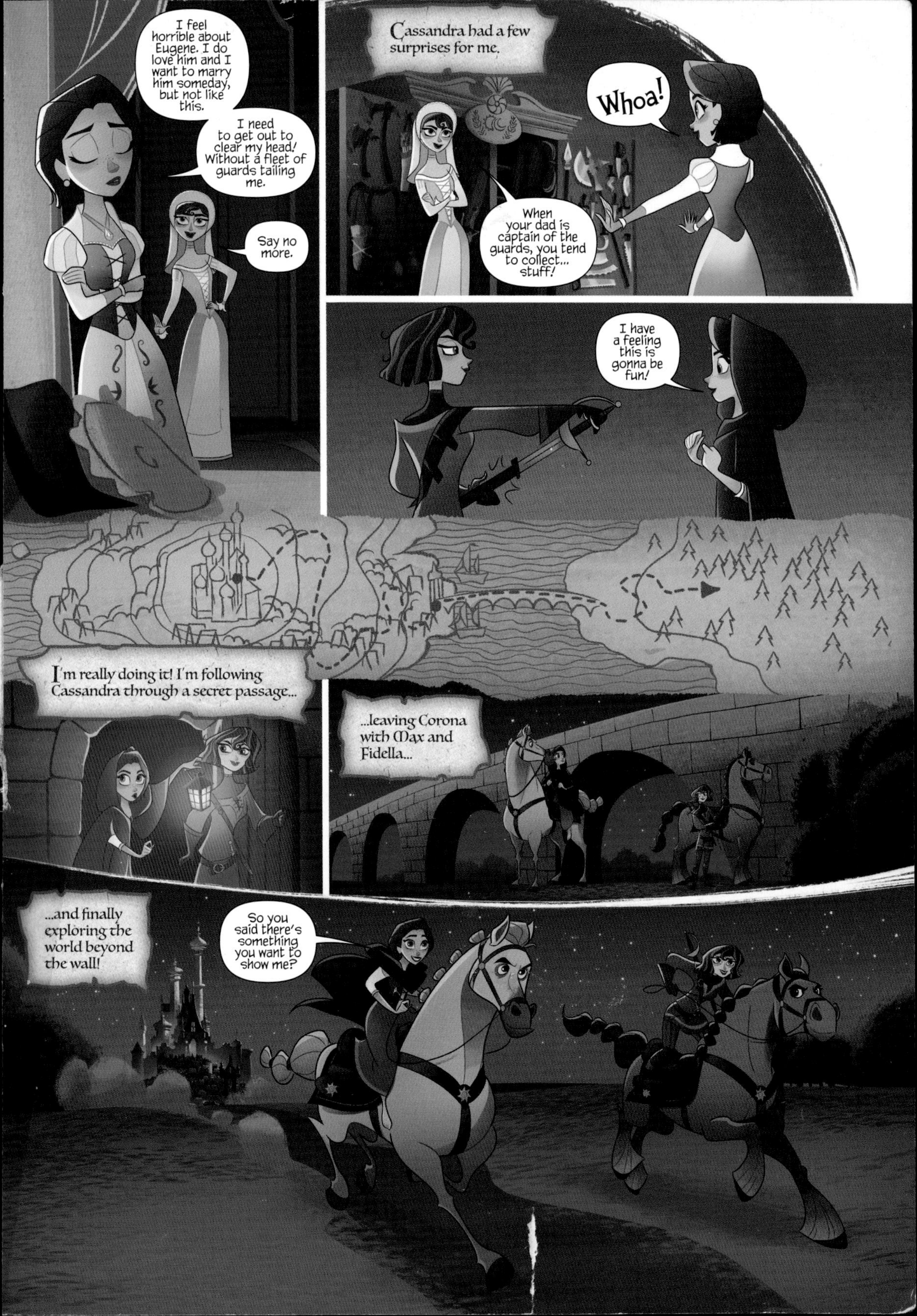
I feel horrible about Eugene. I do love him and I want to marry him someday, but not like this.
I need to get out to clear my head! Without a fleet of guards tailing me.
Say no more.
Cassandra had a few surprises for me.
Whoa!
When your dad is captain of the guards, you tend to collect... stuff!
I have a feeling this is gonna be fun!
I'm really doing it! I'm following Cassandra through a secret passage...
...leaving Corona with Max and Fidella...
...and finally exploring the world beyond the wall!
So you said there's something you want to show me?

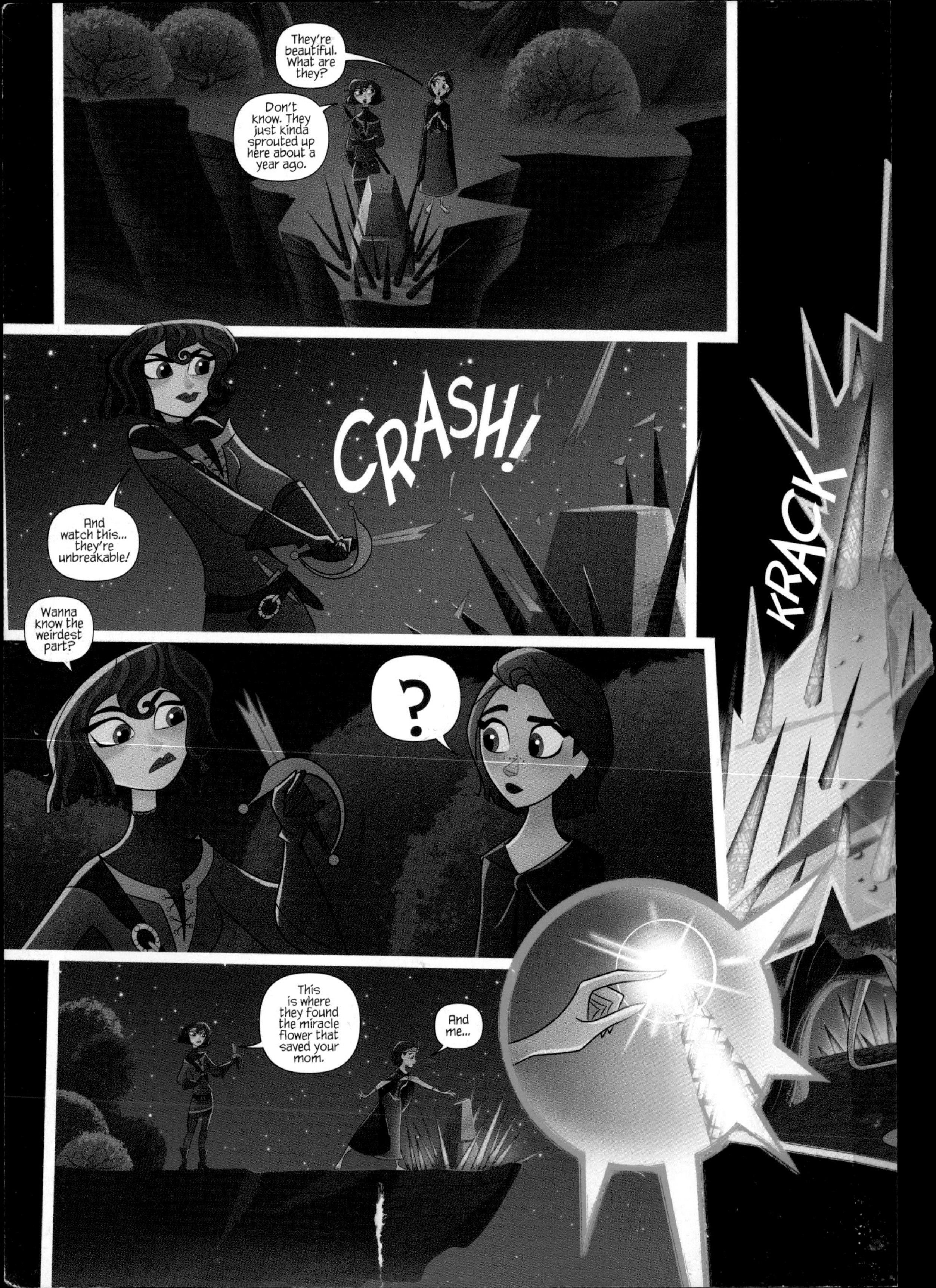
They're beautiful. What are they?
Don't know. They just kinda sprouted up here about a year ago.
And watch this... they're unbreakable!
CRASH!
KRACK
Wanna know the weirdest part?
?
This is where they found the miracle flower that saved your mom.
And me...

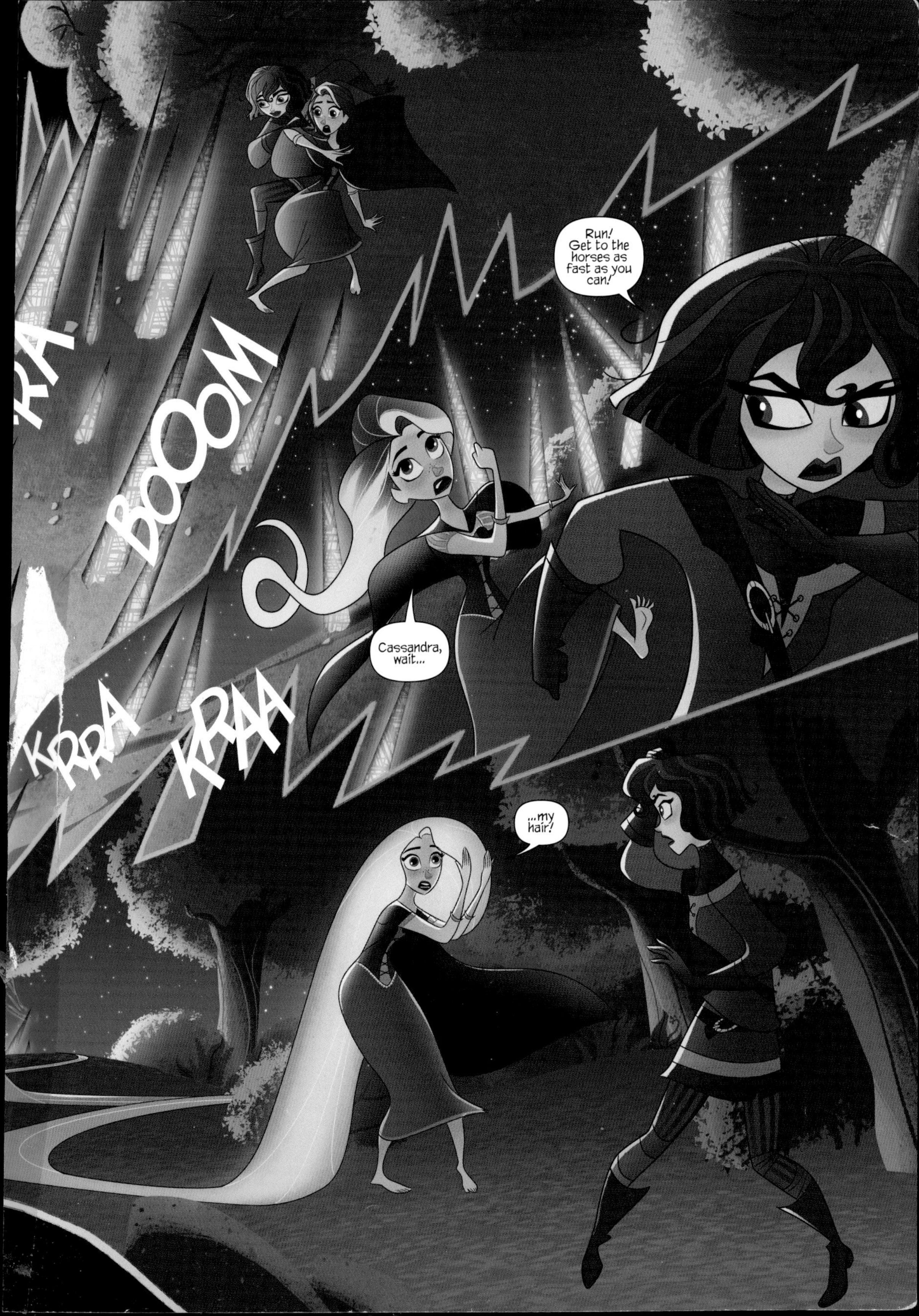
RA
BOOOM
Run! Get to the horses as fast as you can!
Cassandra, wait...
KRRA
KRAA
...my hair!

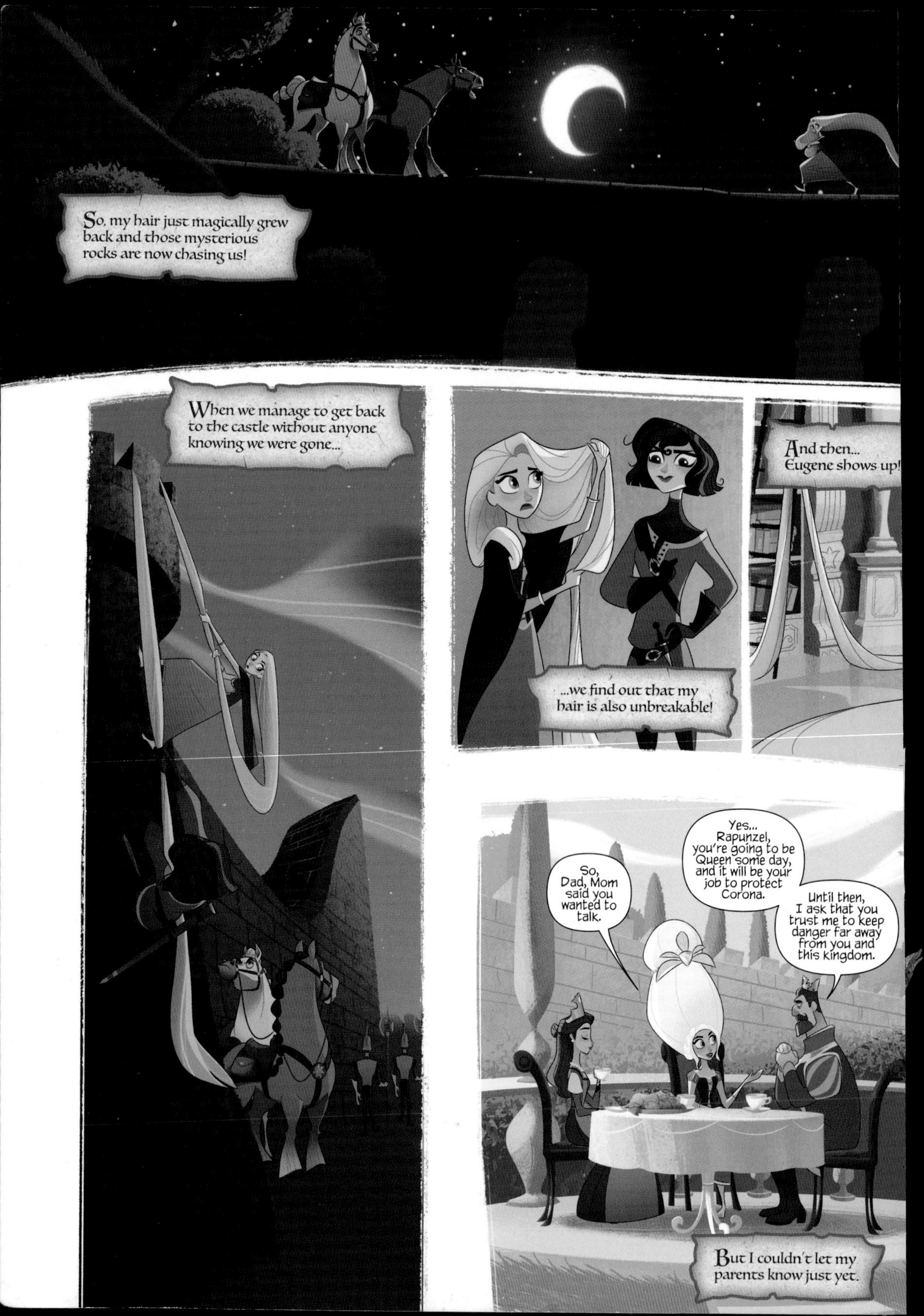
So, my hair just magically grew back and those mysterious rocks are now chasing us!
When we manage to get back to the castle without anyone knowing we were gone...
...we find out that my hair is also unbreakable!
And then... Eugene shows up!
So, Dad, Mom said you wanted to talk.
Yes... Rapunzel, you're going to be Queen some day, and it will be your job to protect Corona.
Until then, I ask that you trust me to keep danger far away from you and this kingdom.
But I couldn't let my parents know just yet.

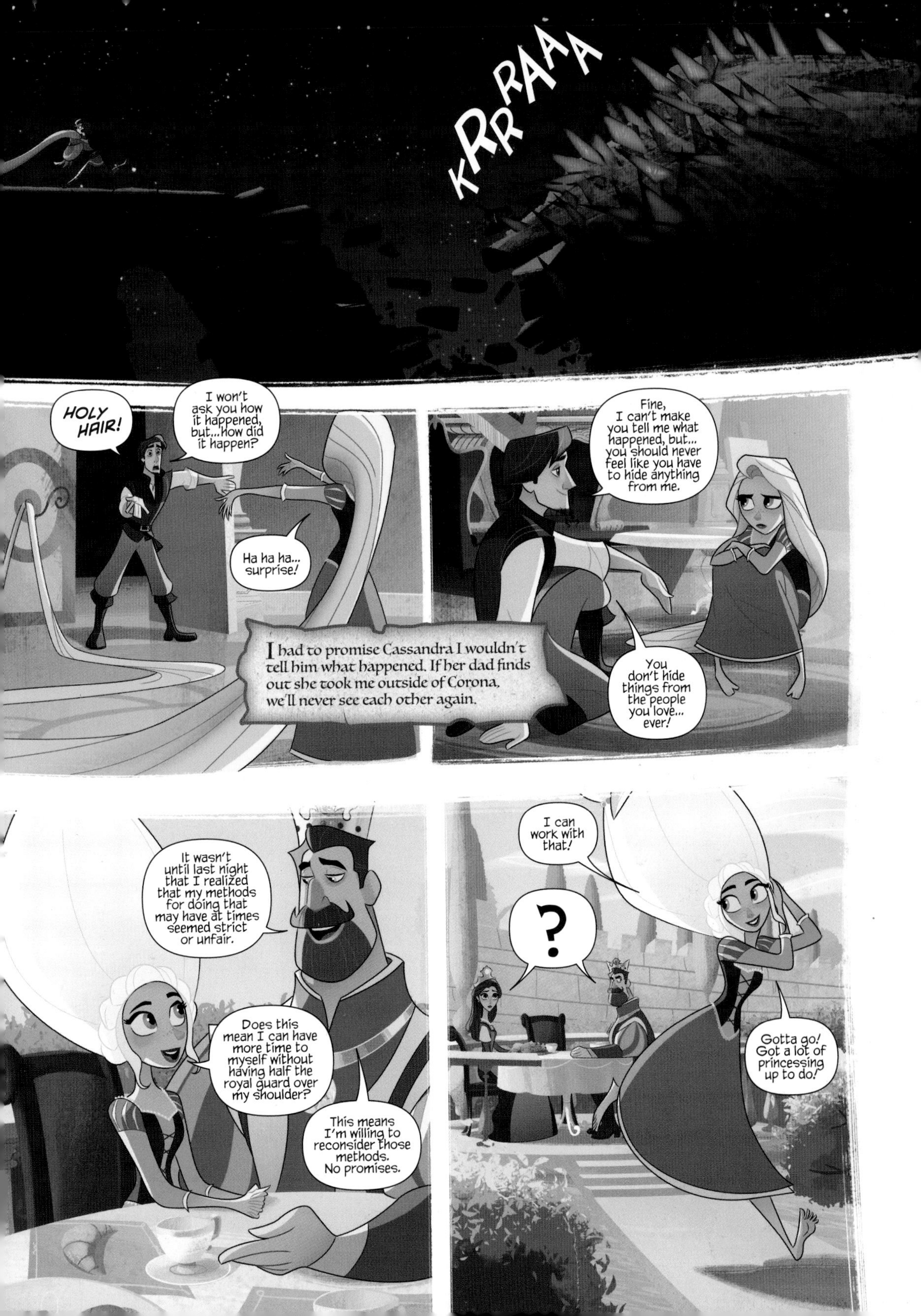
KRRAAAA
HOLY HAIR!
I won't ask you how it happened, but...how did it happen?
Ha ha ha... surprise!
Fine, I can't make you tell me what happened, but... you should never feel like you have to hide anything from me.
I had to promise Cassandra I wouldn't tell him what happened. If her dad finds out she took me outside of Corona, we'll never see each other again.
You don't hide things from the people you love... ever!
It wasn't until last night that I realized that my methods for doing that may have at times seemed strict or unfair.
Does this mean I can have more time to myself without having half the royal guard over my shoulder?
This means I'm willing to reconsider those methods. No promises.
I can work with that!
?
Gotta go! Got a lot of princessing up to do!

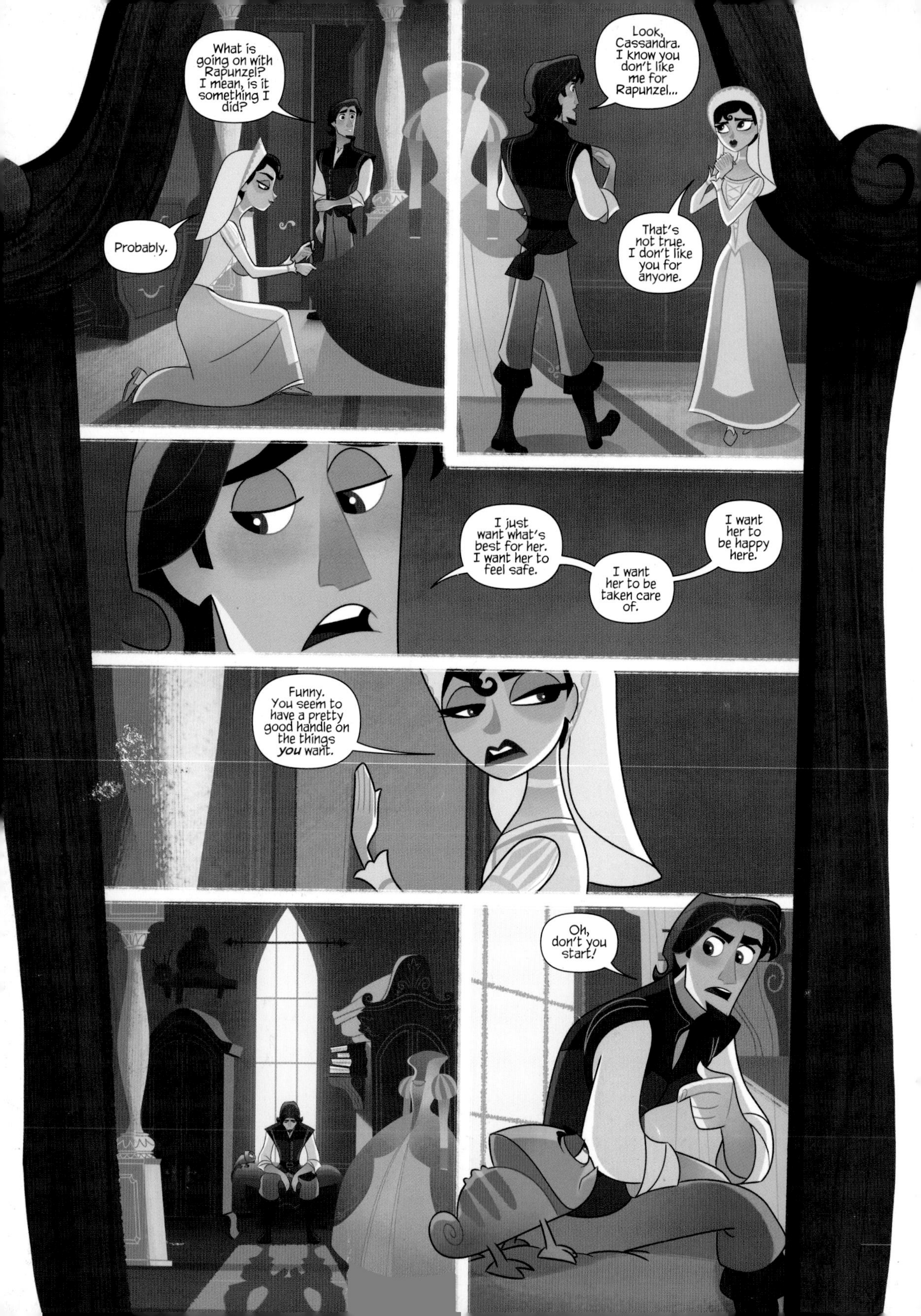
What is going on with Rapunzel? I mean, is it something I did?
Probably.
Look, Cassandra. I know you don't like me for Rapunzel...
That's not true. I don't like you for anyone.
I just want what's best for her. I want her to feel safe.
I want her to be taken care of.
I want her to be happy here.
Funny. You seem to have a pretty good handle on the things *you* want.
Oh, don't you start!

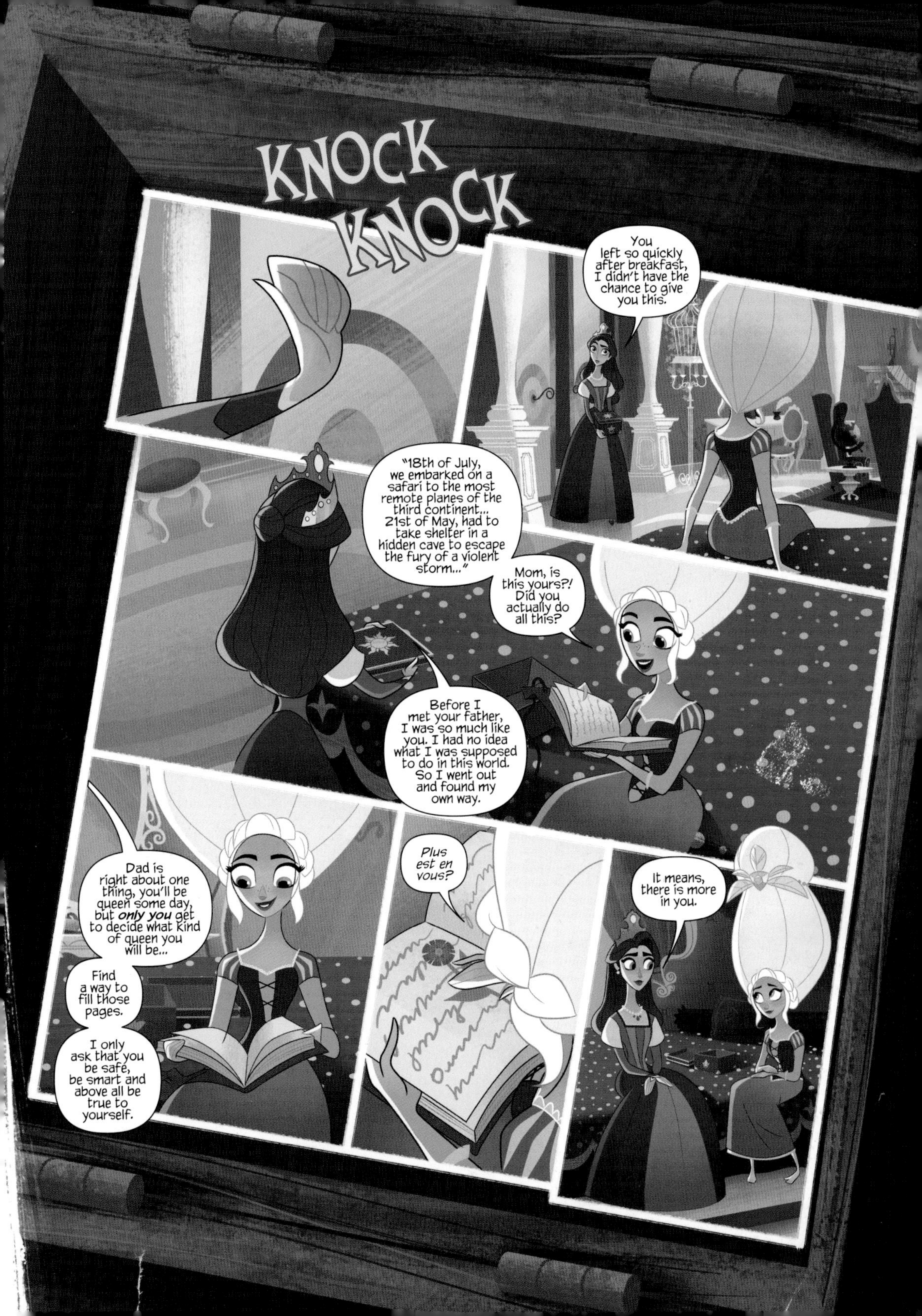
KNOCK KNOCK
You left so quickly after breakfast, I didn't have the chance to give you this.
"18th of July, we embarked on a safari to the most remote planes of the third continent... 21st of May, had to take shelter in a hidden cave to escape the fury of a violent storm..."
Mom, is this yours?! Did you actually do all this?
Before I met your father, I was so much like you. I had no idea what I was supposed to do in this world. So I went out and found my own way.
Dad is right about one thing, you'll be queen some day, but ***only you*** get to decide what kind of queen you will be...
Find a way to fill those pages.
I only ask that you be safe, be smart and above all be true to yourself.
Plus est en vous?
It means, there is more in you.

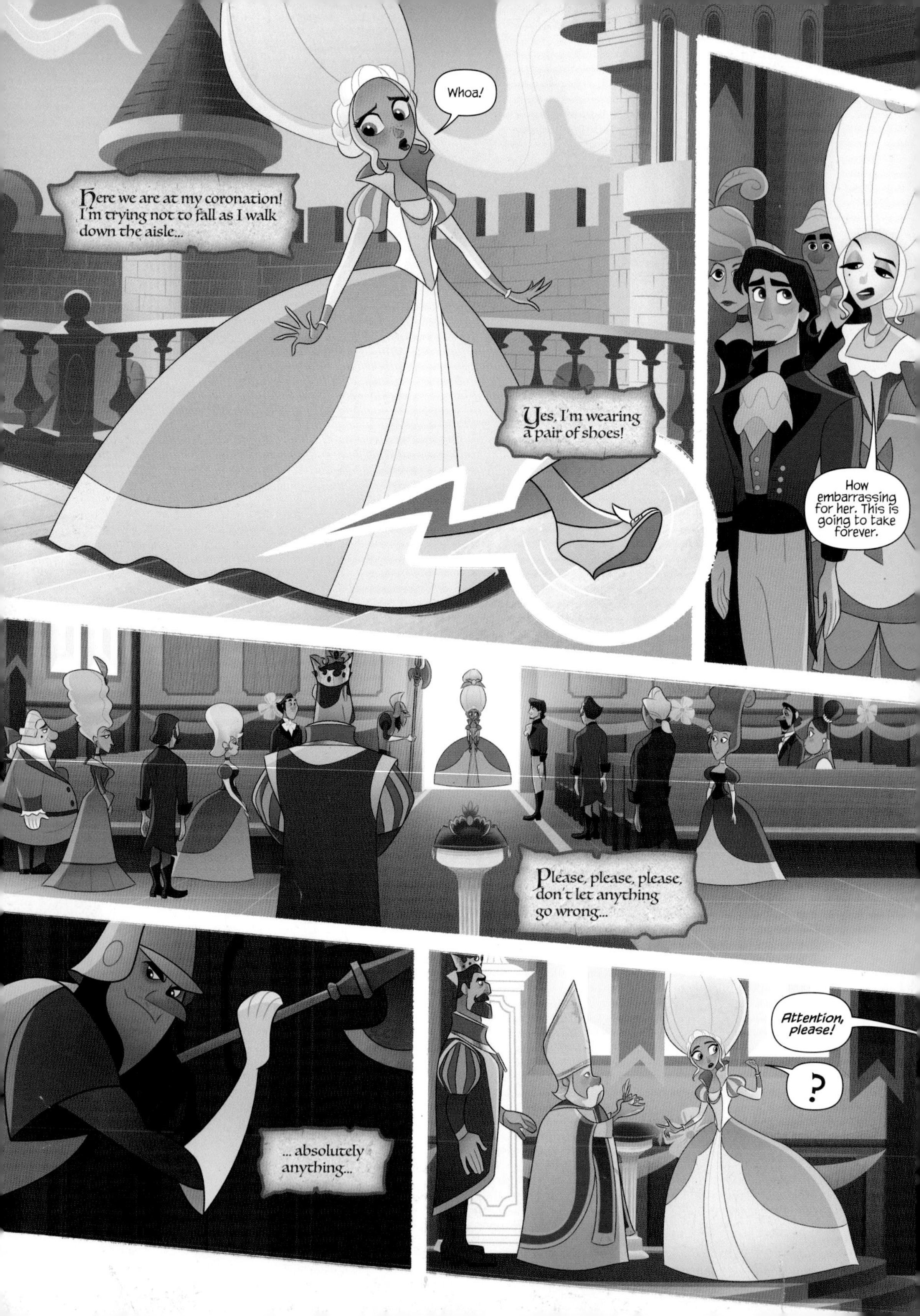
Whoa!
Here we are at my coronation! I'm trying not to fall as I walk down the aisle...
Yes, I'm wearing a pair of shoes!
How embarrassing for her. This is going to take forever.
Please, please, please, don't let anything go wrong...
... absolutely anything...
Attention, please!
?

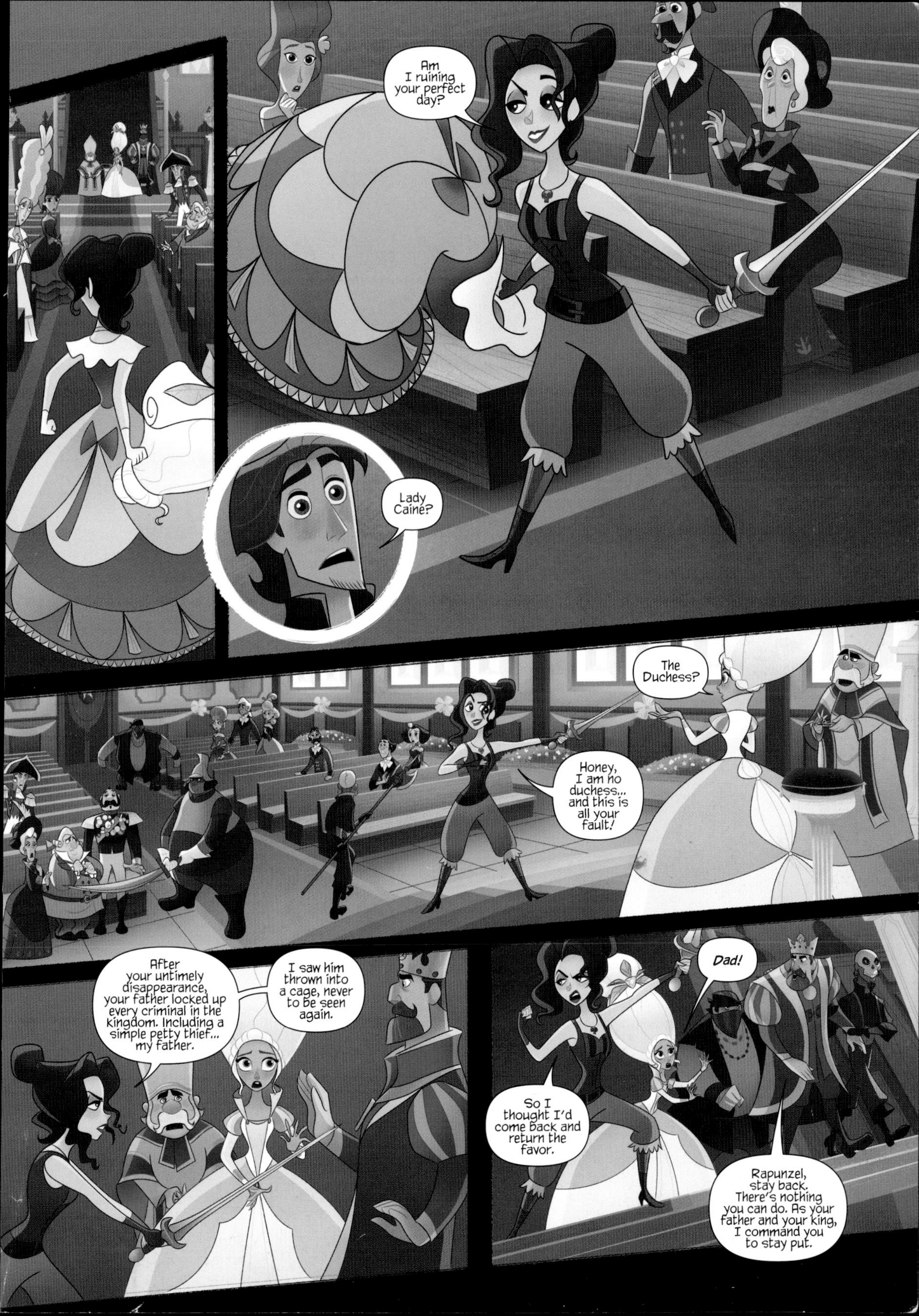
Am I ruining your perfect day?
Lady Caine?
The Duchess?
Honey, I am no duchess... and this is all your fault!
After your untimely disappearance, your father locked up every criminal in the kingdom. Including a simple petty thief... my father.
I saw him thrown into a cage, never to be seen again.
So I thought I'd come back and return the favor.
Dad!
Rapunzel, stay back. There's nothing you can do. As your father and your king, I command you to stay put.

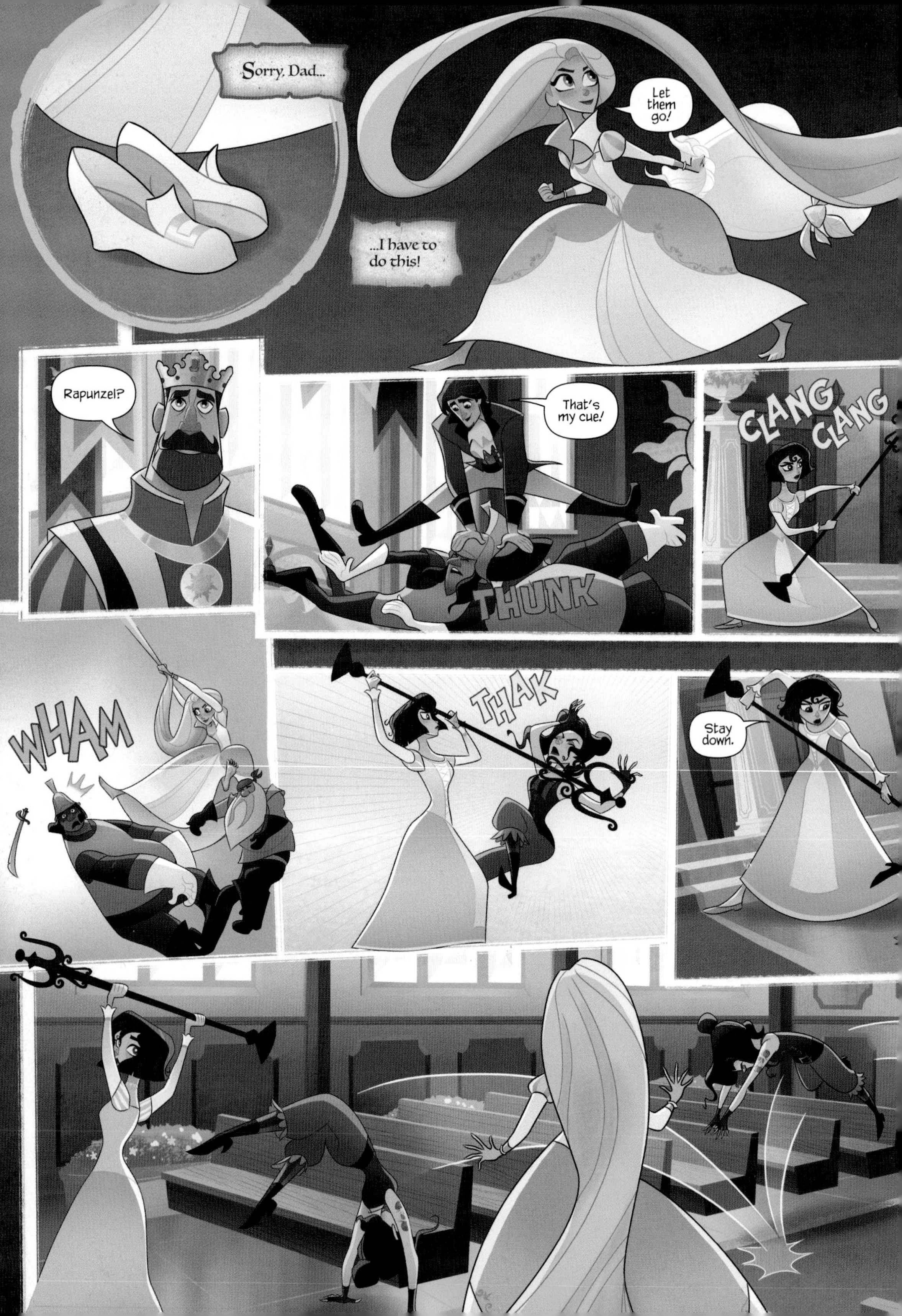
Sorry, Dad...
Let them go!
...I have to do this!
Rapunzel?
That's my cue!
THUNK
CLANG CLANG
WHAM
THAK
Stay down.

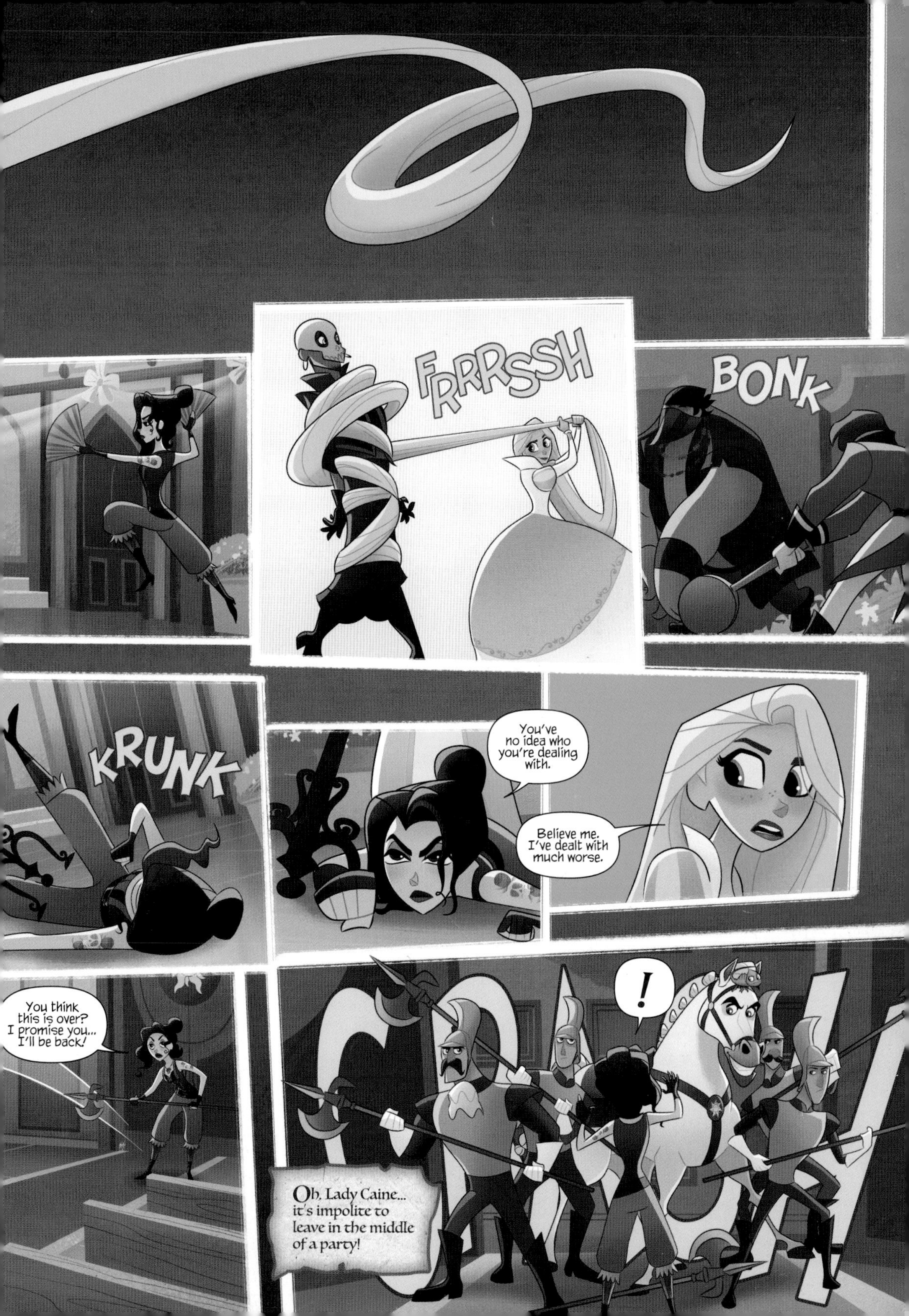
FRRRSSH
BONK
KRUNK
You've no idea who you're dealing with.
Believe me. I've dealt with much worse.
You think this is over? I promise you... I'll be back!
!
Oh, Lady Caine... it's impolite to leave in the middle of a party!

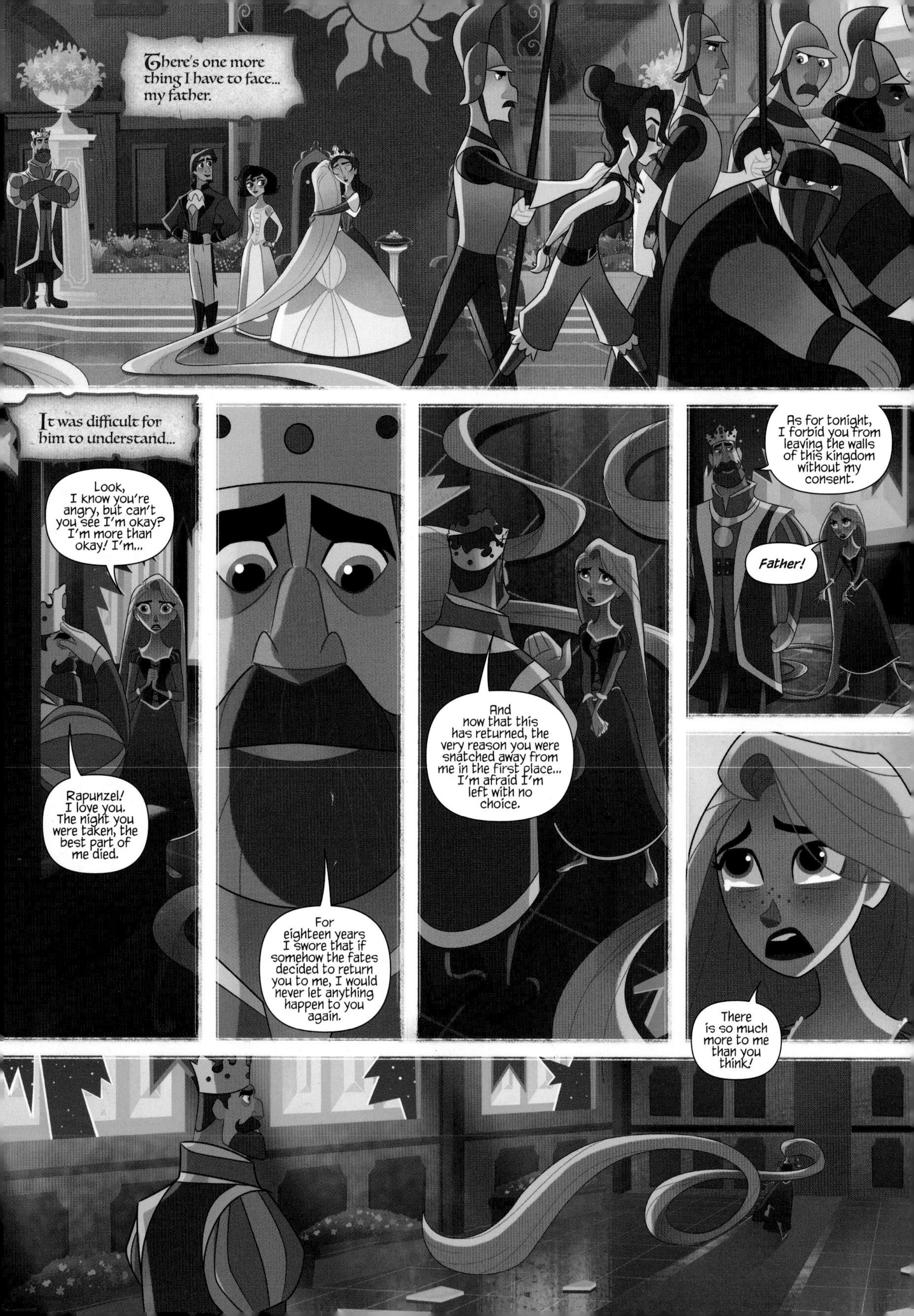
There's one more thing I have to face... my father.
It was difficult for him to understand...
Look, I know you're angry, but can't you see I'm okay? I'm more than okay! I'm...
Rapunzel! I love you. The night you were taken, the best part of me died.
For eighteen years I swore that if somehow the fates decided to return you to me, I would never let anything happen to you again.
And now that this has returned, the very reason you were snatched away from me in the first place... I'm afraid I'm left with no choice.
As for tonight, I forbid you from leaving the walls of this kingdom without my consent.
Father!
There is so much more to me than you think!

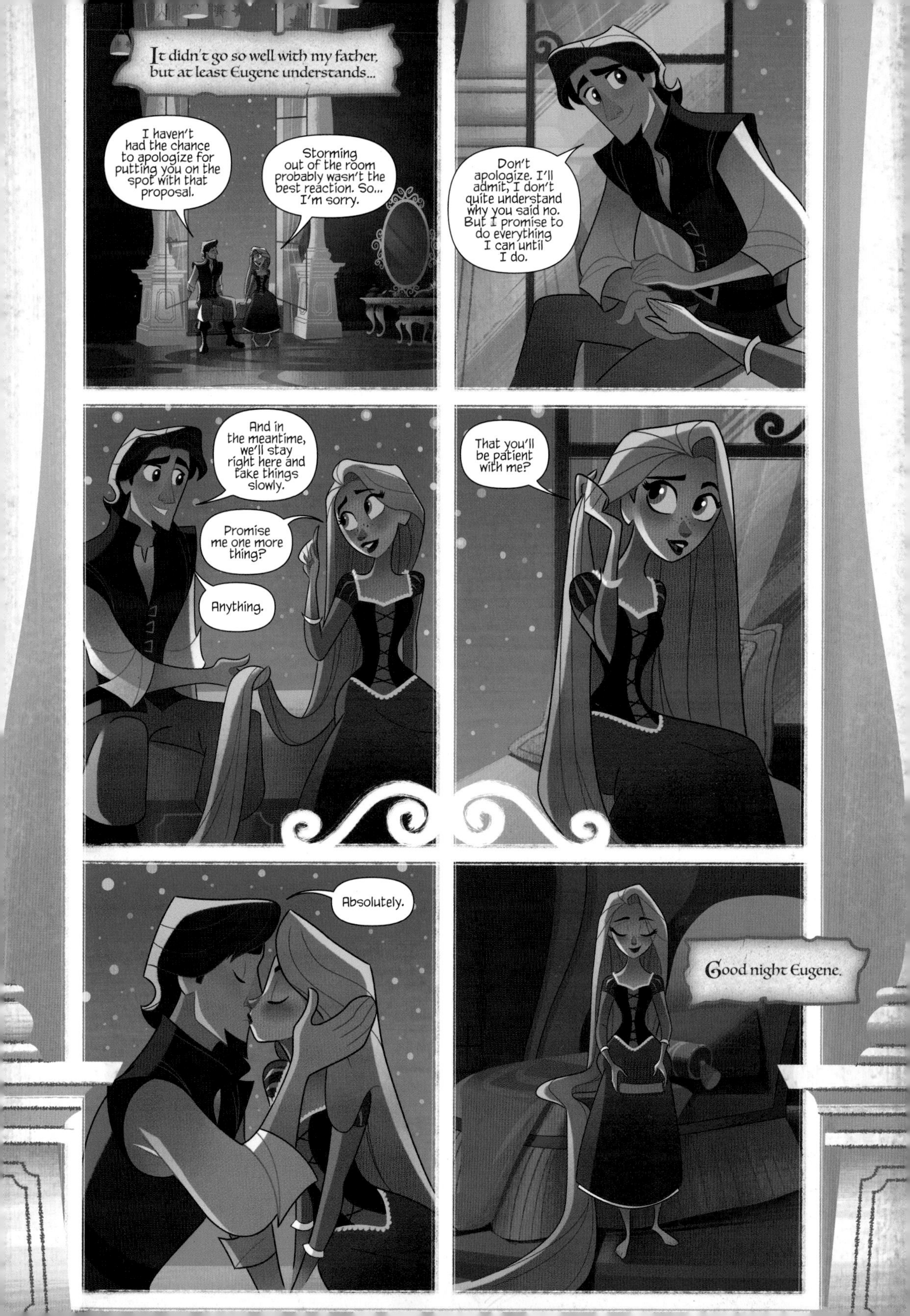

It didn't go so well with my father, but at least Eugene understands...
I haven't had the chance to apologize for putting you on the spot with that proposal.
Storming out of the room probably wasn't the best reaction. So... I'm sorry.
Don't apologize. I'll admit, I don't quite understand why you said no. But I promise to do everything I can until I do.
And in the meantime, we'll stay right here and take things slowly.
Promise me one more thing?
Anything.
That you'll be patient with me?
Absolutely.
Good night Eugene.

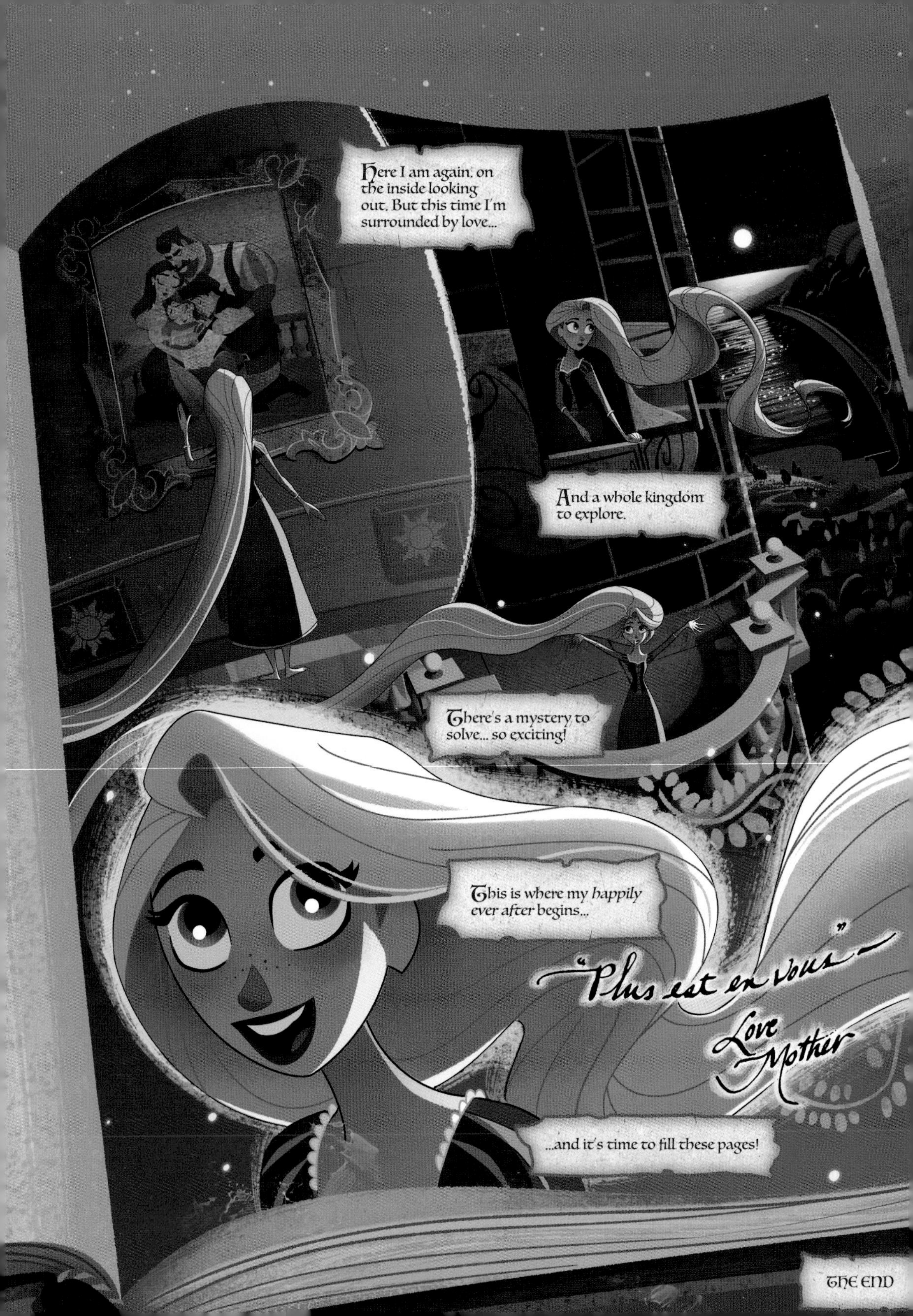

Here I am again, on the inside looking out. But this time I'm surrounded by love...
And a whole kingdom to explore.
There's a mystery to solve... so exciting!
This is where my *happily ever after* begins...
"Plus est en vous" – Love Mother
...and it's time to fill these pages!
THE END

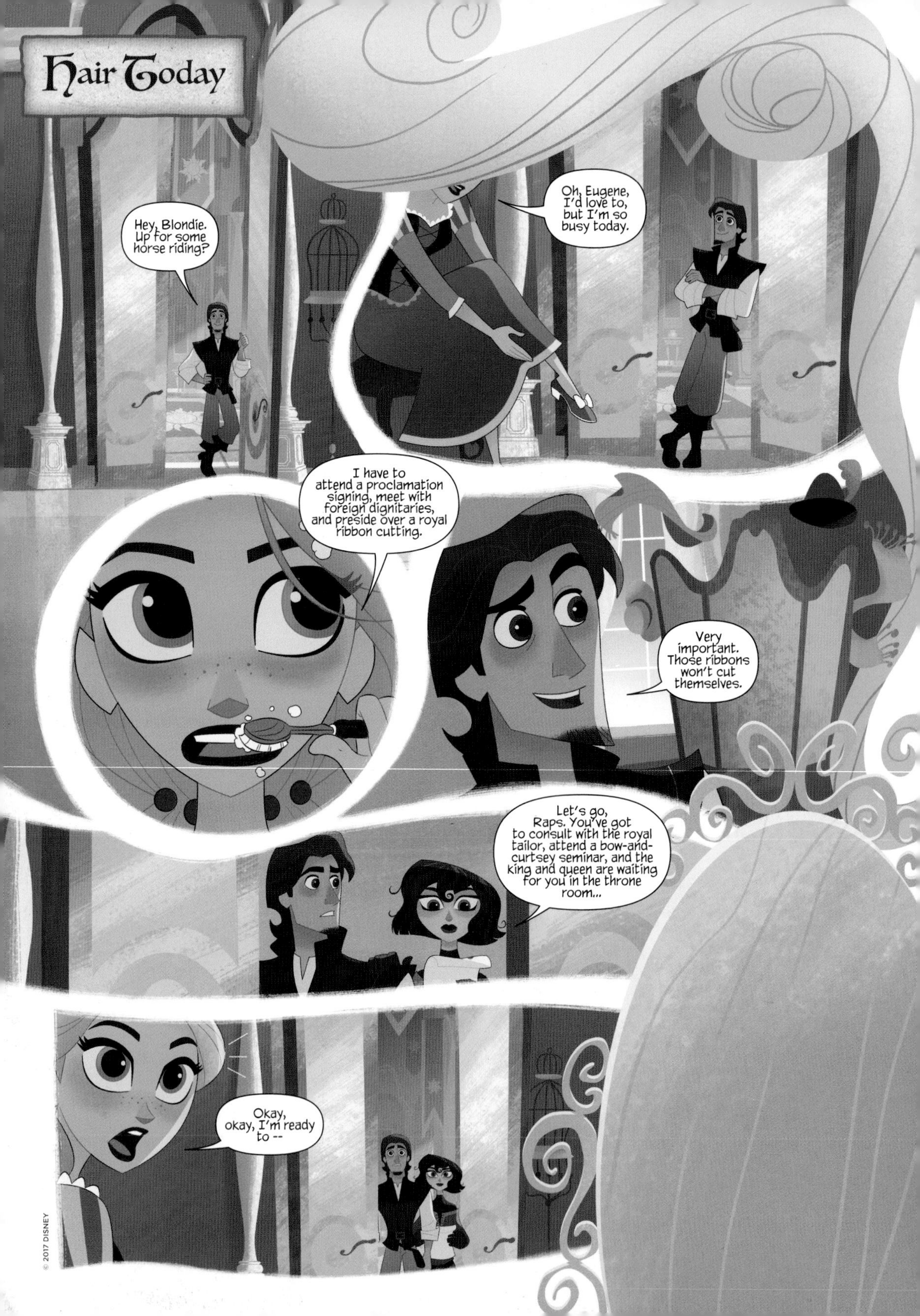
Hair Today
Hey, Blondie. Up for some horse riding?
Oh, Eugene, I'd love to, but I'm so busy today.
I have to attend a proclamation signing, meet with foreign dignitaries, and preside over a royal ribbon cutting.
Very important. Those ribbons won't cut themselves.
Let's go, Raps. You've got to consult with the royal tailor, attend a bow-and-curtsey seminar, and the king and queen are waiting for you in the throne room...
Okay, okay, I'm ready to --

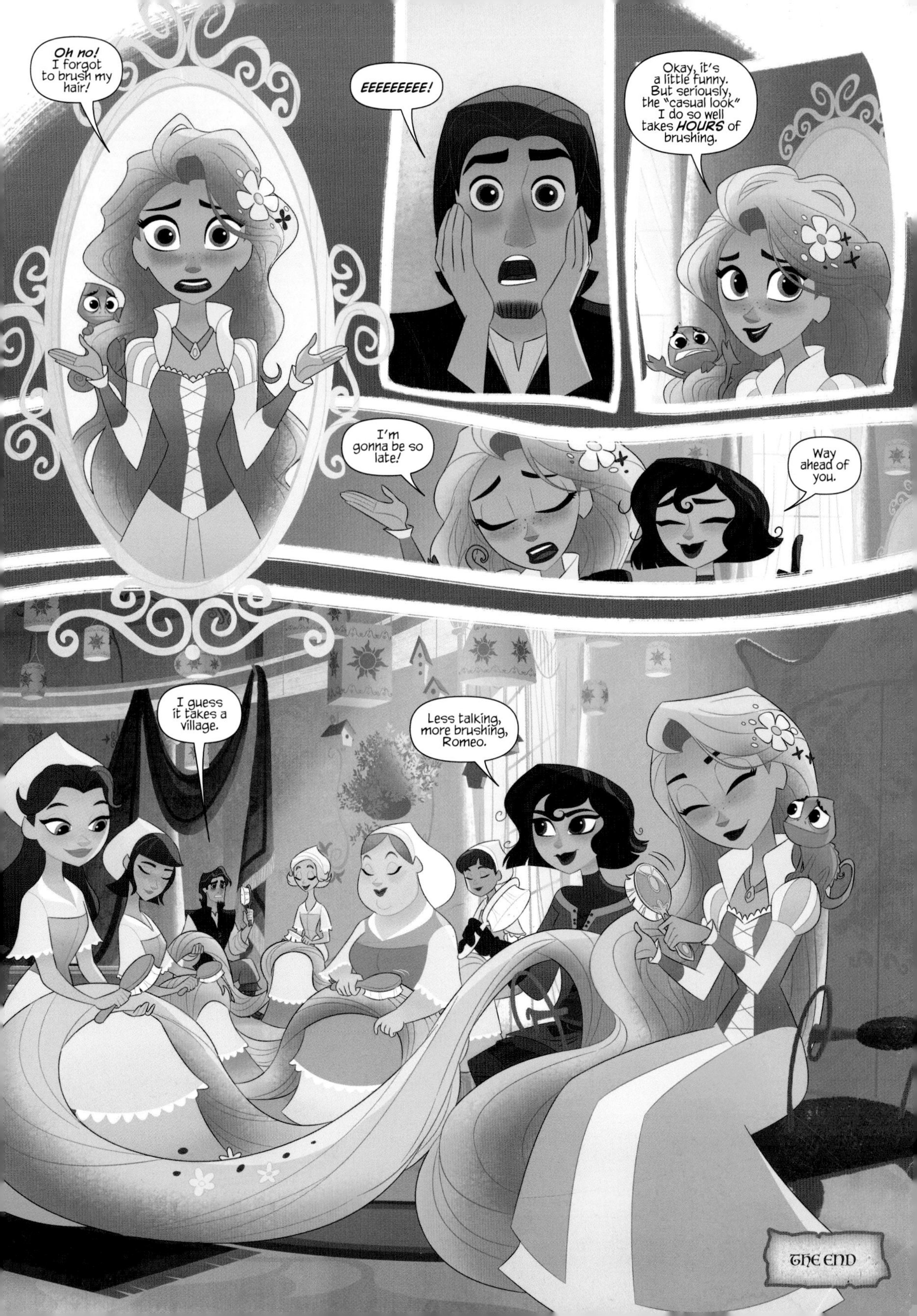

Oh no! I forgot to brush my hair!
EEEEEEEEE!
Okay, it's a little funny. But seriously, the "casual look" I do so well takes HOURS of brushing.
I'm gonna be so late!
Way ahead of you.
I guess it takes a village.
Less talking, more brushing, Romeo.
THE END

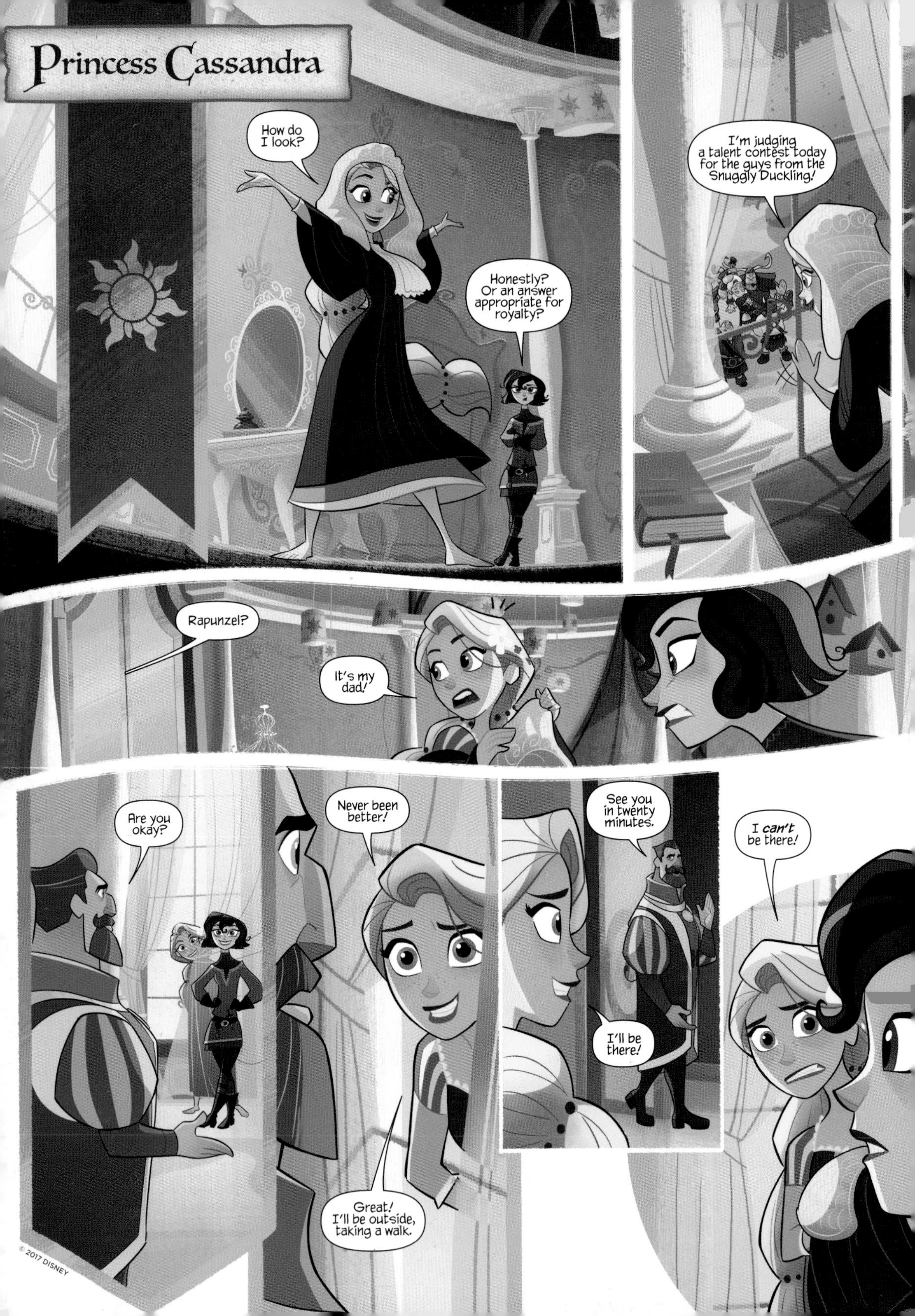
Princess Cassandra
How do I look?
Honestly? Or an answer appropriate for royalty?
I'm judging a talent contest today for the guys from the Snuggly Duckling!
Rapunzel?
It's my dad!
Are you okay?
Never been better!
Great! I'll be outside, taking a walk.
See you in twenty minutes.
I'll be there!
I *can't* be there!

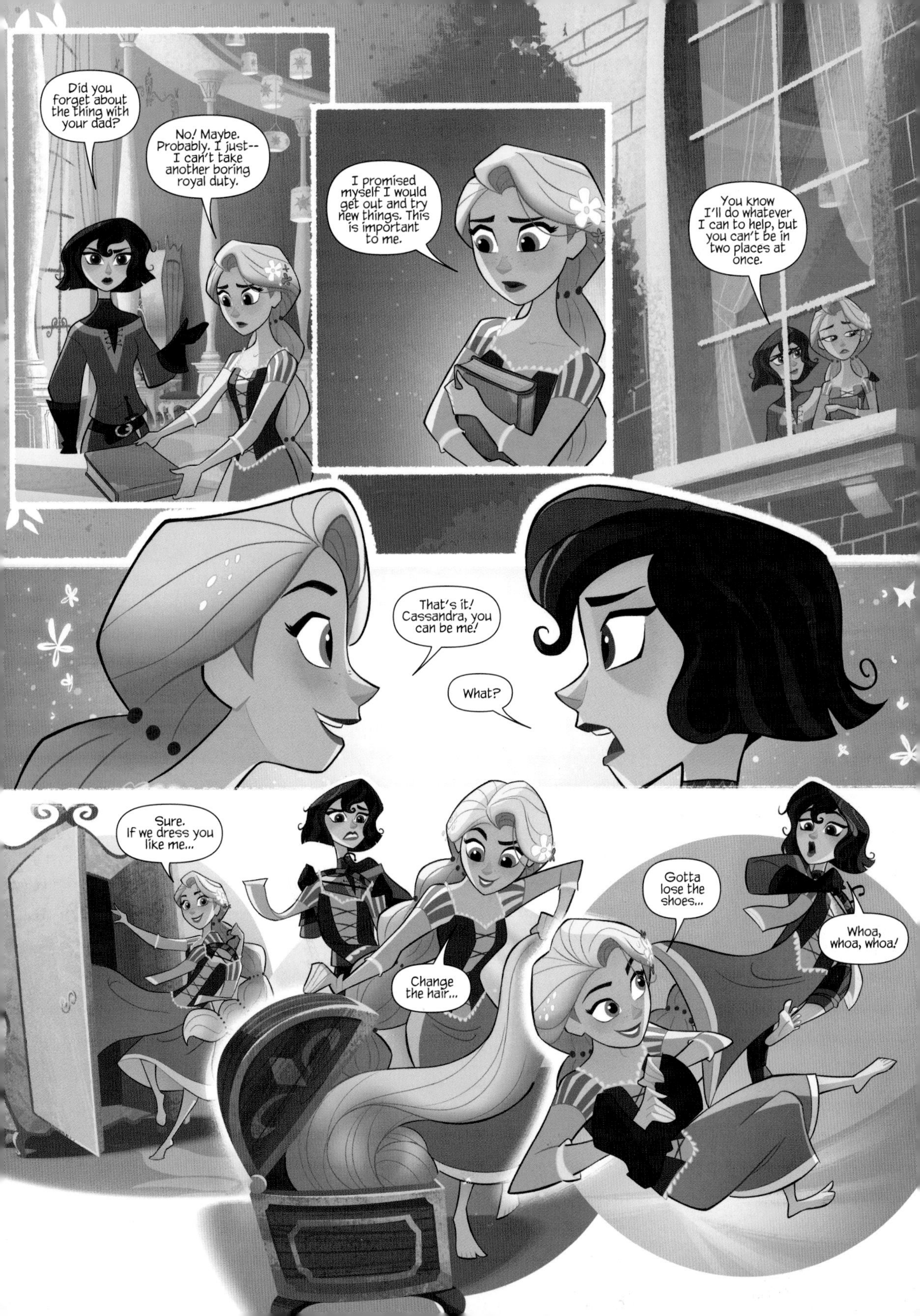

Did you forget about the thing with your dad?
No! Maybe. Probably. I just-- I can't take another boring royal duty.
I promised myself I would get out and try new things. This is important to me.
You know I'll do whatever I can to help, but you can't be in two places at once.
That's it! Cassandra, you can be me!
What?
Sure. If we dress you like me...
Change the hair...
Gotta lose the shoes...
Whoa, whoa, whoa!

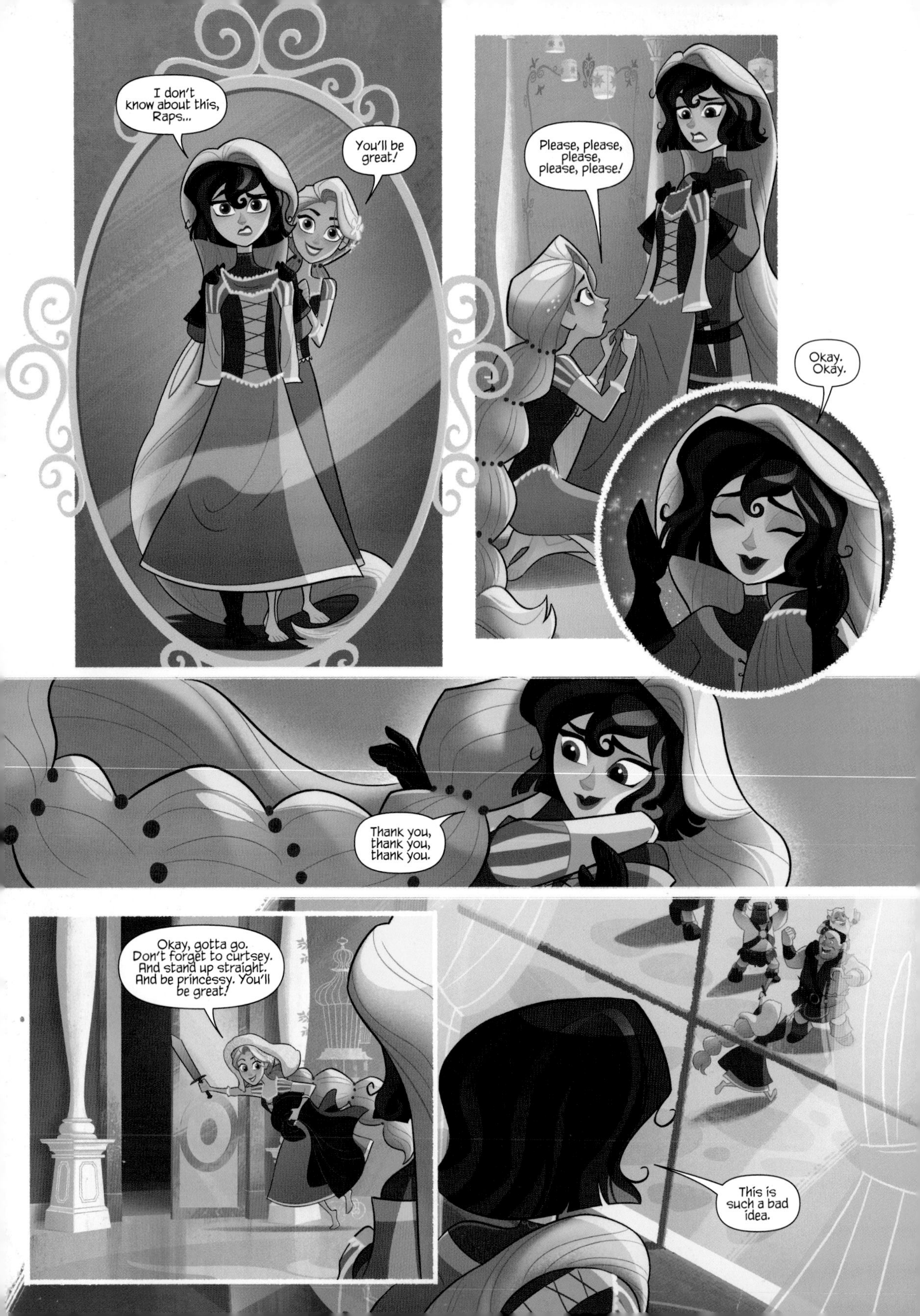
I don't know about this, Raps...
You'll be great!
Please, please, please, please, please!
Okay. Okay.
Thank you, thank you, thank you.
Okay, gotta go. Don't forget to curtsey. And stand up straight. And be princessy. You'll be great!
This is such a bad idea.

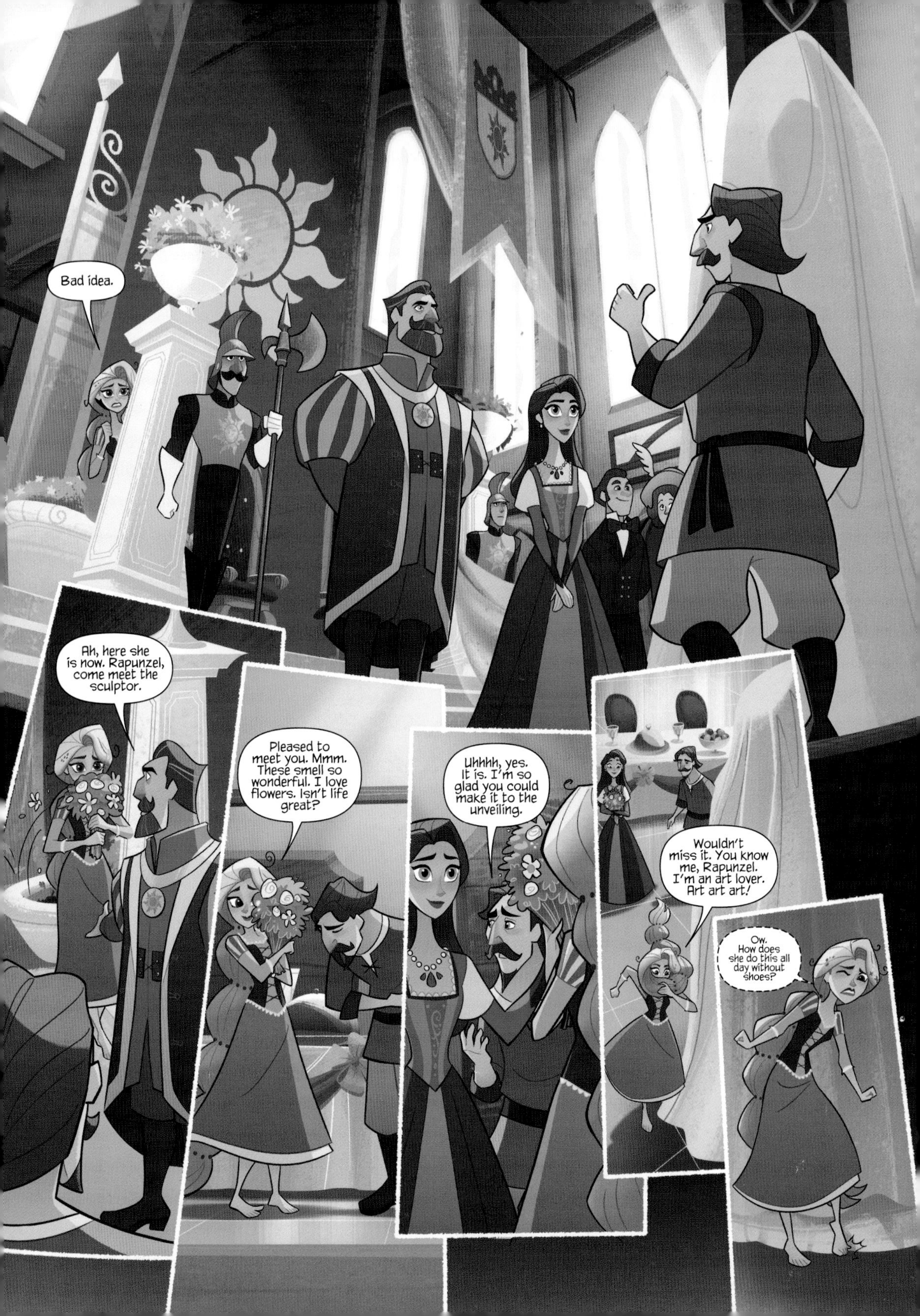
Bad idea.
Ah, here she is now. Rapunzel, come meet the sculptor.
Pleased to meet you. Mmm. These smell so wonderful. I love flowers. Isn't life great?
Uhhhh, yes. It is. I'm so glad you could make it to the unveiling.
Wouldn't miss it. You know me, Rapunzel. I'm an art lover. Art art art!
Ow. How does she do this all day without shoes?

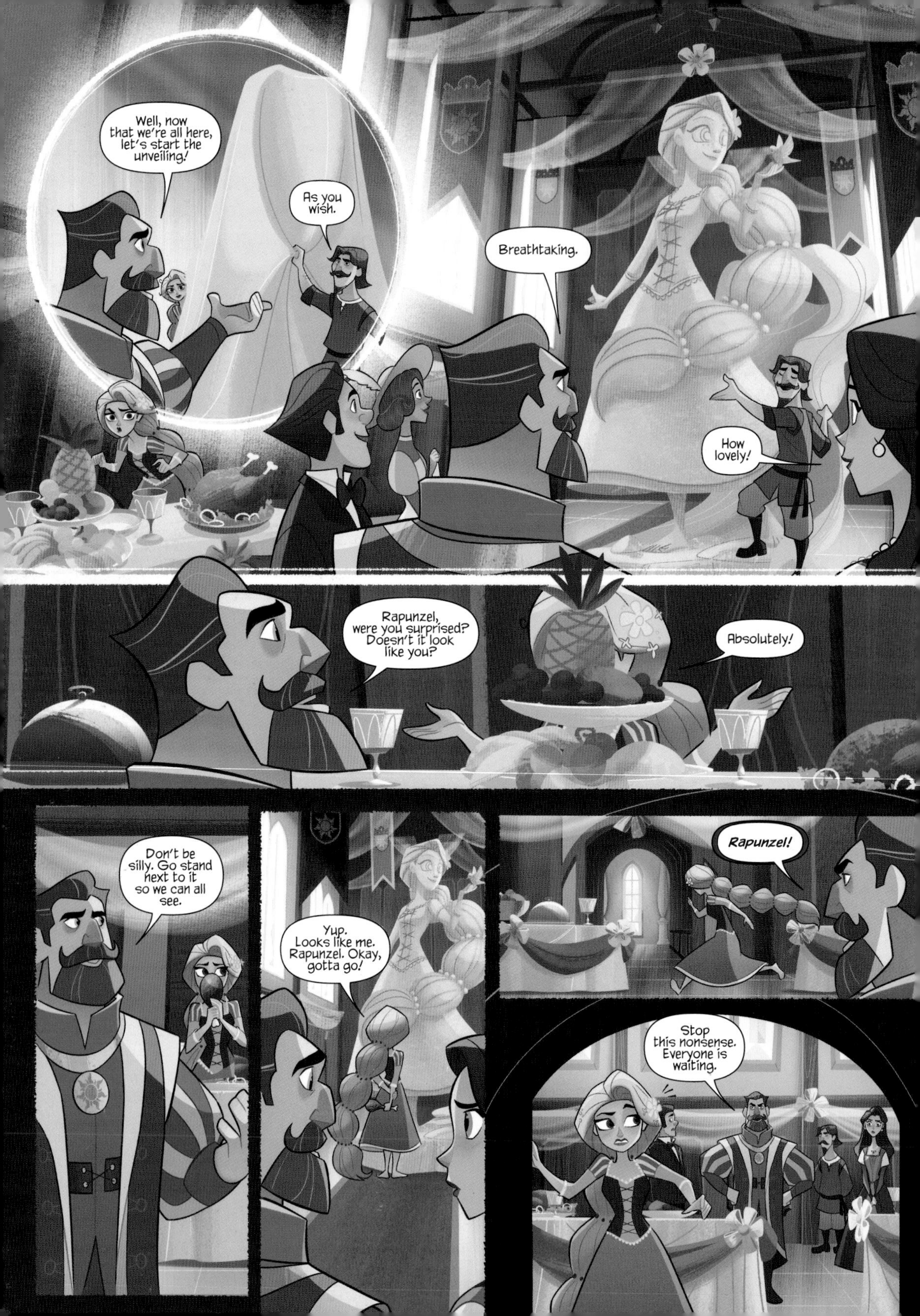
Well, now that we're all here, let's start the unveiling!
As you wish.
Breathtaking.
How lovely!
Rapunzel, were you surprised? Doesn't it look like you?
Absolutely!
Don't be silly. Go stand next to it so we can all see.
Yup. Looks like me. Rapunzel. Okay, gotta go!
Rapunzel!
Stop this nonsense. Everyone is waiting.

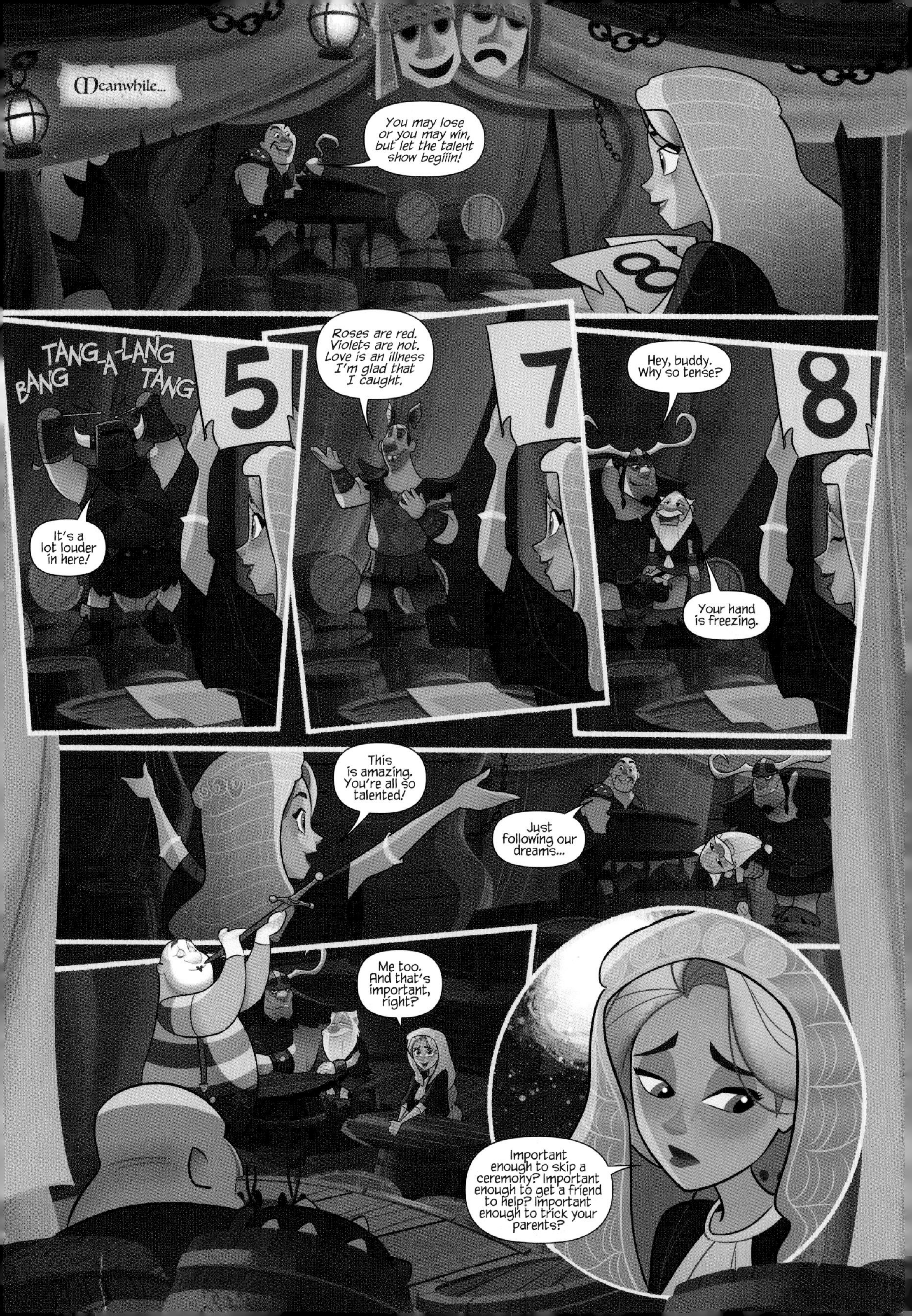

Meanwhile...
You may lose or you may win, but let the talent show begiiin!
TANG-A-LANG BANG TANG
5
It's a lot louder in here!
Roses are red. Violets are not. Love is an illness I'm glad that I caught.
7
Hey, buddy. Why so tense?
8
Your hand is freezing.
This is amazing. You're all so talented!
Just following our dreams...
Me too. And that's important, right?
Important enough to skip a ceremony? Important enough to get a friend to help? Important enough to trick your parents?

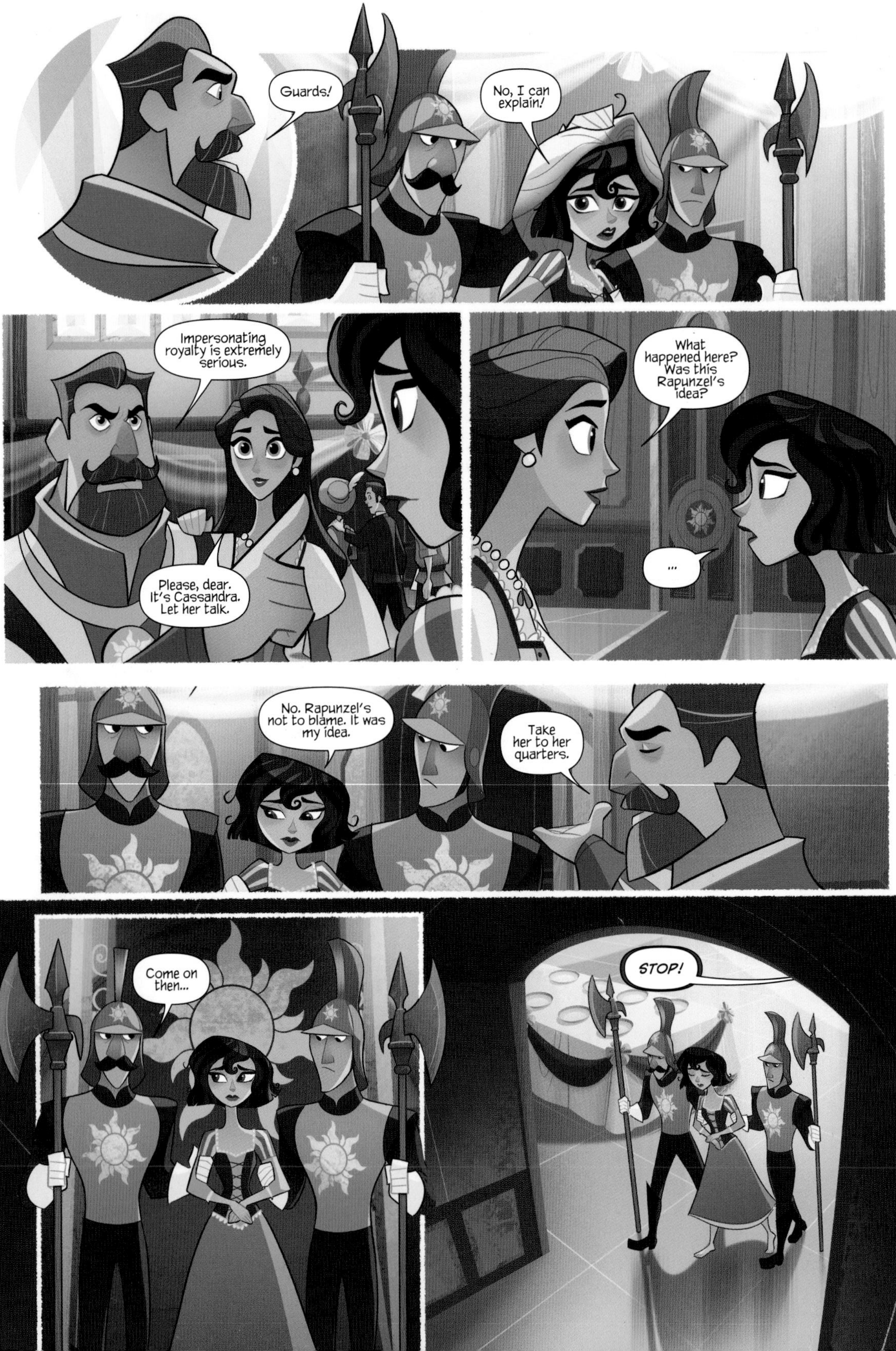
Guards!
No, I can explain!
Impersonating royalty is extremely serious.
Please, dear. It's Cassandra. Let her talk.
What happened here? Was this Rapunzel's idea?
...
No. Rapunzel's not to blame. It was my idea.
Take her to her quarters.
Come on then...
STOP!

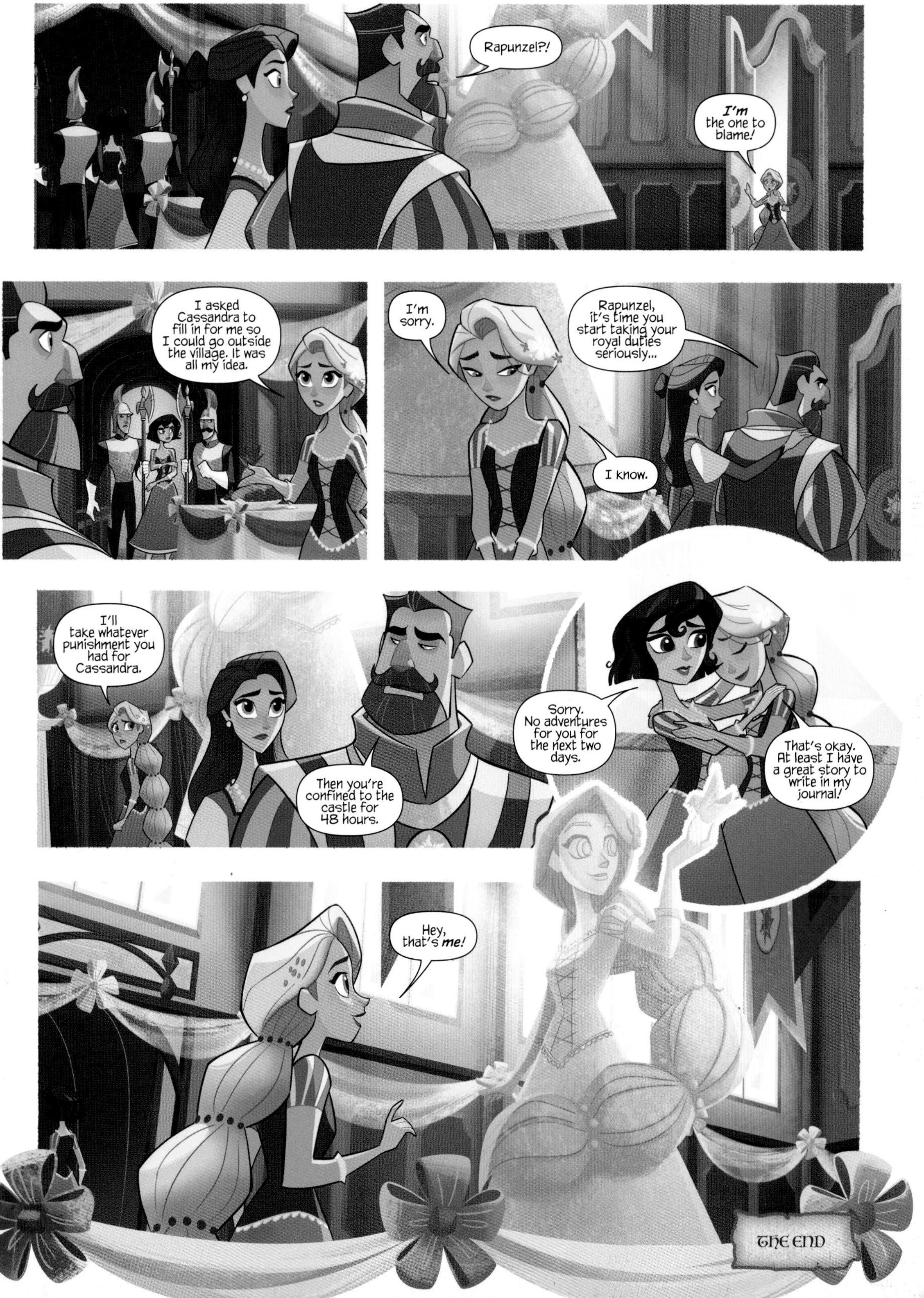

Rapunzel?!
I'm the one to blame!
I asked Cassandra to fill in for me so I could go outside the village. It was all my idea.
I'm sorry.
Rapunzel, it's time you start taking your royal duties seriously...
I know.
I'll take whatever punishment you had for Cassandra.
Then you're confined to the castle for 48 hours.
Sorry. No adventures for you for the next two days.
That's okay. At least I have a great story to write in my journal!
Hey, that's me!
THE END

Greetings

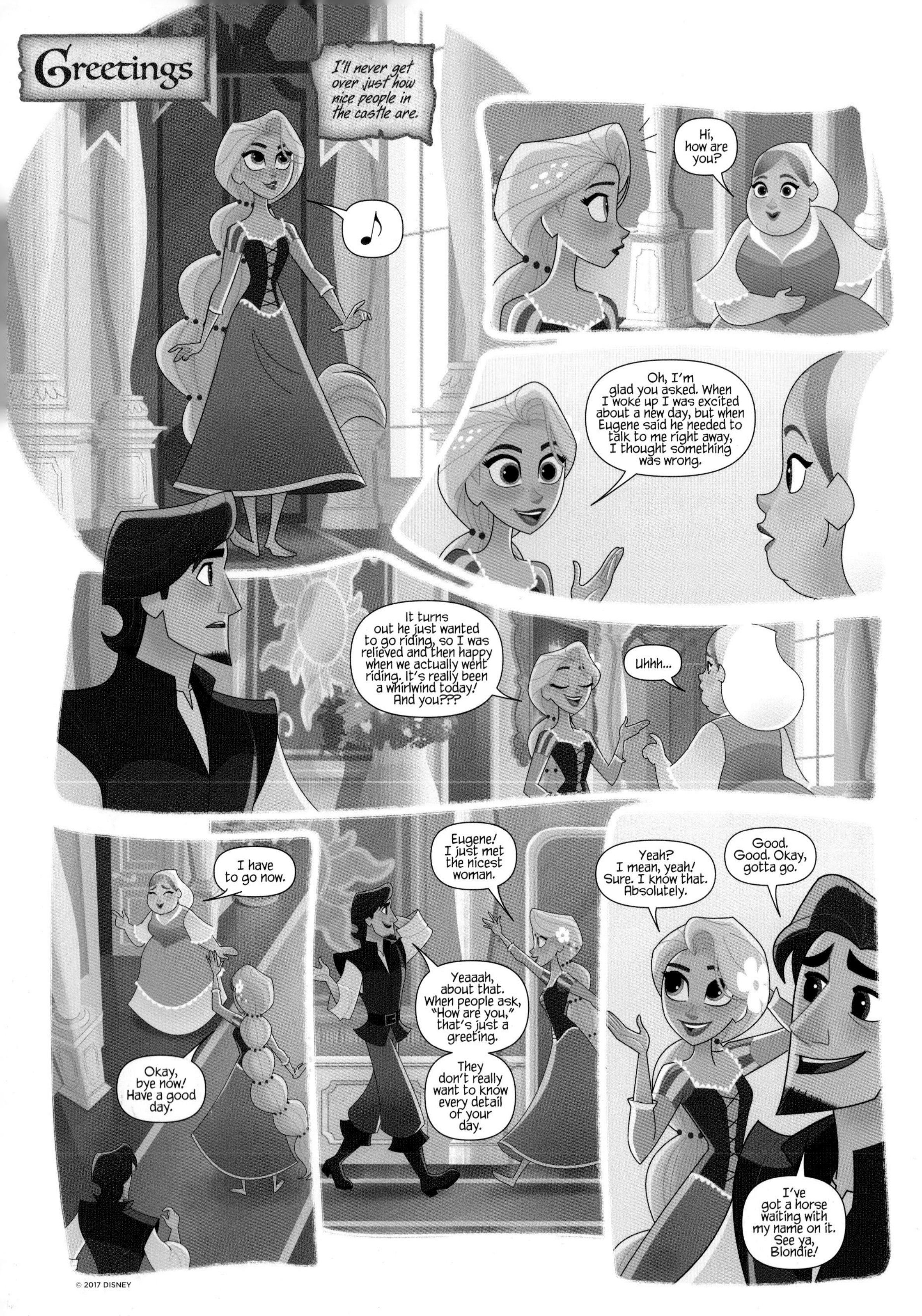

I'll never get over just how nice people in the castle are.
♪
Hi, how are you?
Oh, I'm glad you asked. When I woke up I was excited about a new day, but when Eugene said he needed to talk to me right away, I thought something was wrong.
It turns out he just wanted to go riding, so I was relieved and then happy when we actually went riding. It's really been a whirlwind today! And you???
Uhhh...
I have to go now.
Okay, bye now! Have a good day.
Eugene! I just met the nicest woman.
Yeaaah, about that. When people ask, "How are you," that's just a greeting.
They don't really want to know every detail of your day.
Yeah? I mean, yeah! Sure. I know that. Absolutely.
Good. Good. Okay, gotta go.
I've got a horse waiting with my name on it. See ya, Blondie!

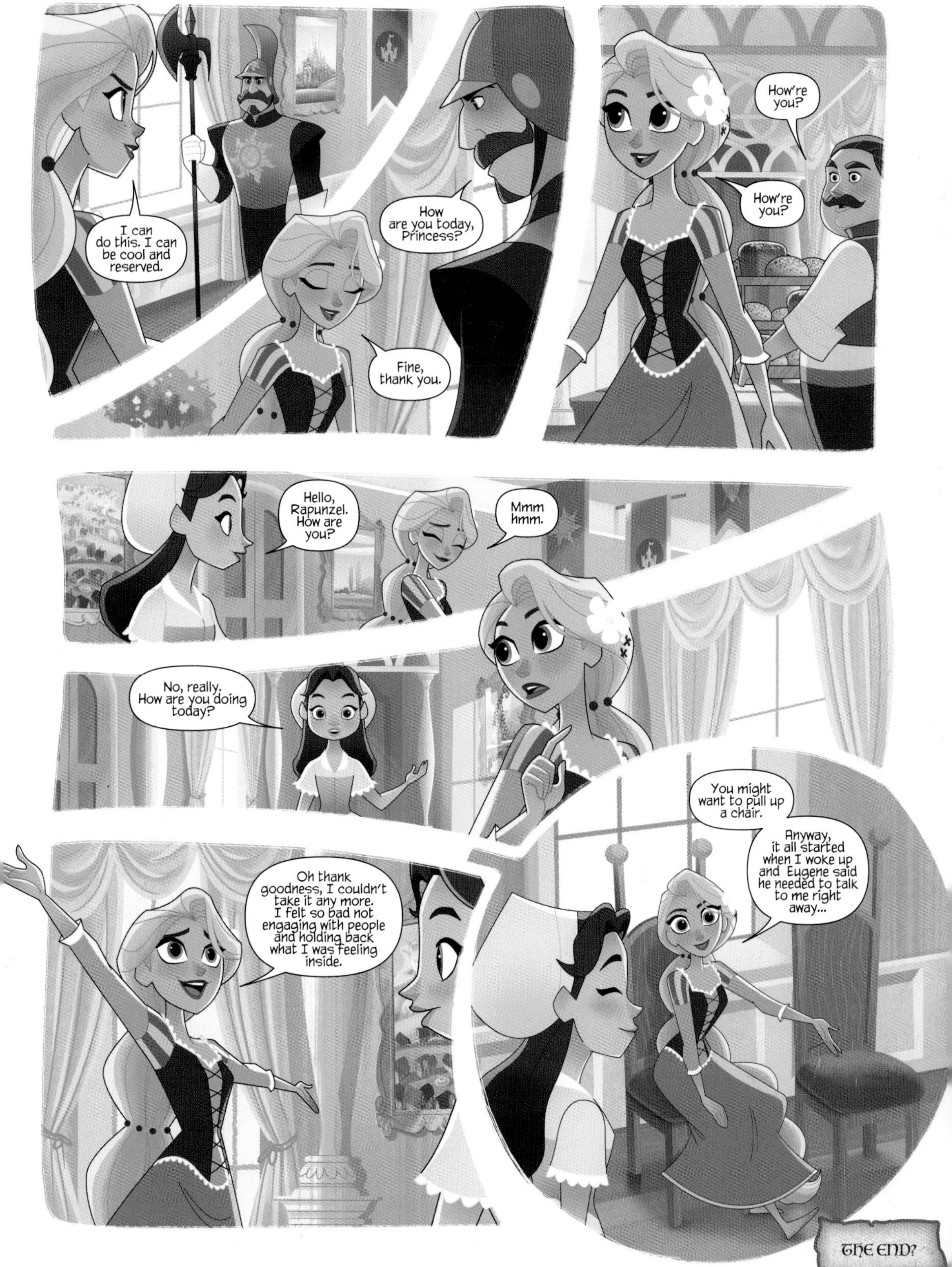
I can do this. I can be cool and reserved.
How are you today, Princess?
Fine, thank you.
How're you?
How're you?
Hello, Rapunzel. How are you?
Mmm hmm.
No, really. How are you doing today?
Oh thank goodness, I couldn't take it any more. I felt so bad not engaging with people and holding back what I was feeling inside.
You might want to pull up a chair.
Anyway, it all started when I woke up and Eugene said he needed to talk to me right away...
THE END?

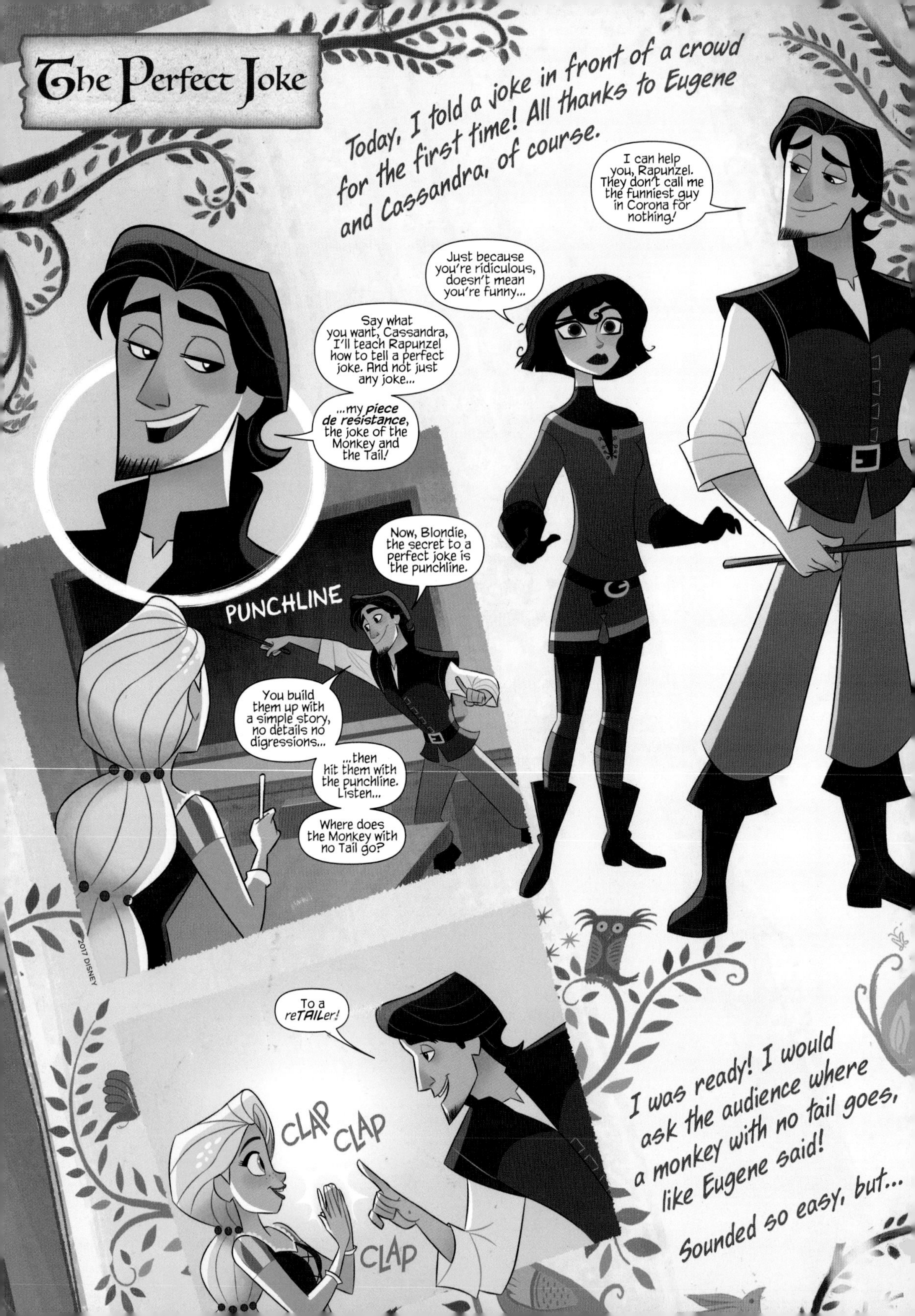

The Perfect Joke
Today, I told a joke in front of a crowd for the first time! All thanks to Eugene and Cassandra, of course.
I can help you, Rapunzel. They don't call me the funniest guy in Corona for nothing!
Just because you're ridiculous, doesn't mean you're funny...
Say what you want, Cassandra, I'll teach Rapunzel how to tell a perfect joke. And not just any joke...
...my *piece de resistance*, the joke of the Monkey and the Tail!
Now, Blondie, the secret to a perfect joke is the punchline.
PUNCHLINE
You build them up with a simple story, no details no digressions...
...then hit them with the punchline. Listen...
Where does the Monkey with no Tail go?
To a *reTAILer!*
CLAP CLAP
CLAP
I was ready! I would ask the audience where a monkey with no tail goes, like Eugene said!
Sounded so easy, but...

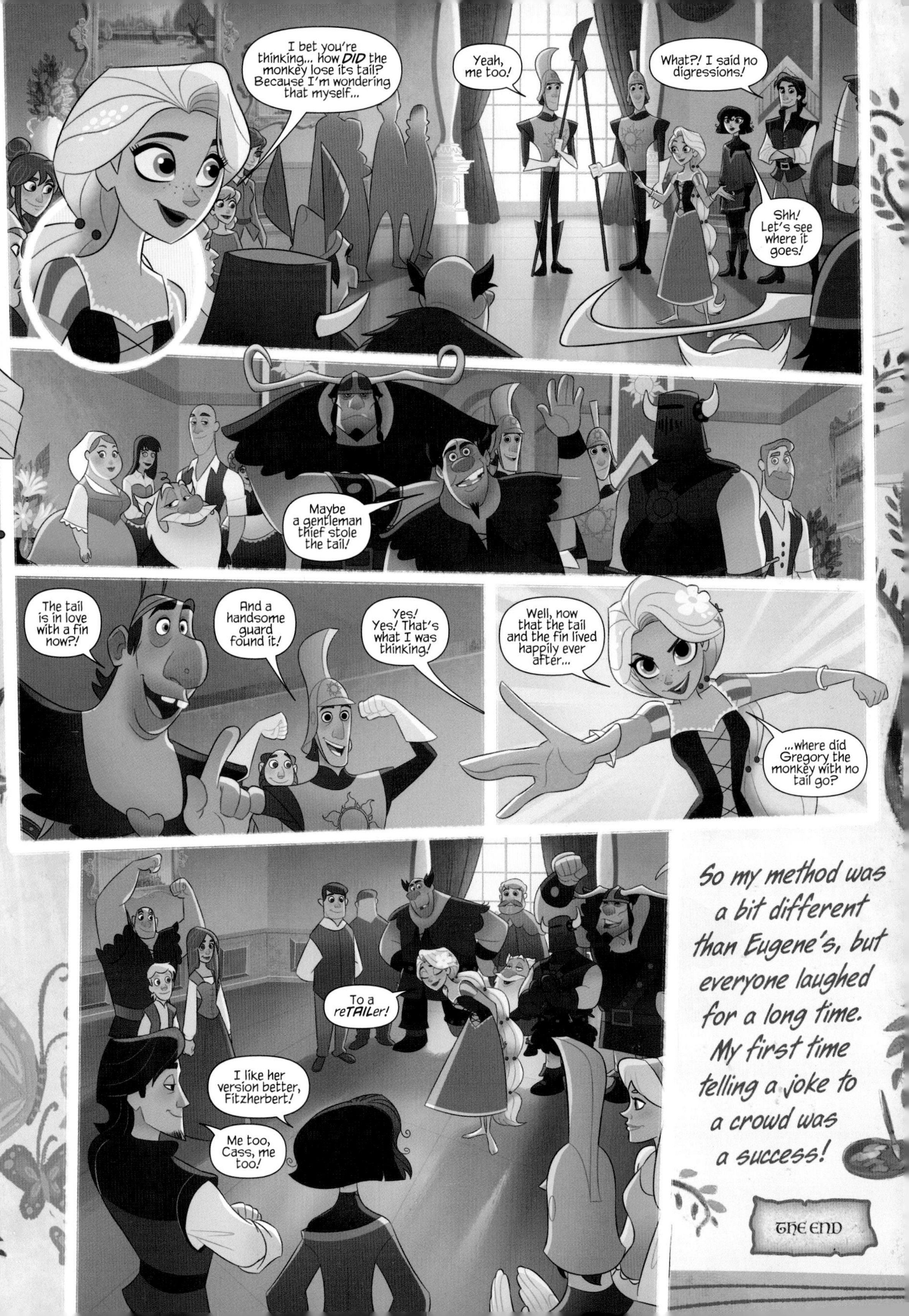

I bet you're thinking... how DID the monkey lose its tail? Because I'm wondering that myself...
Yeah, me too!
What?! I said no digressions!
Shh! Let's see where it goes!
Maybe a gentleman thief stole the tail!
The tail is in love with a fin now?!
And a handsome guard found it!
Yes! Yes! That's what I was thinking!
Well, now that the tail and the fin lived happily ever after...
...where did Gregory the monkey with no tail go?
To a reTAILer!
I like her version better, Fitzherbert!
Me too, Cass, me too!
So my method was a bit different than Eugene's, but everyone laughed for a long time. My first time telling a joke to a crowd was a success!
THE END

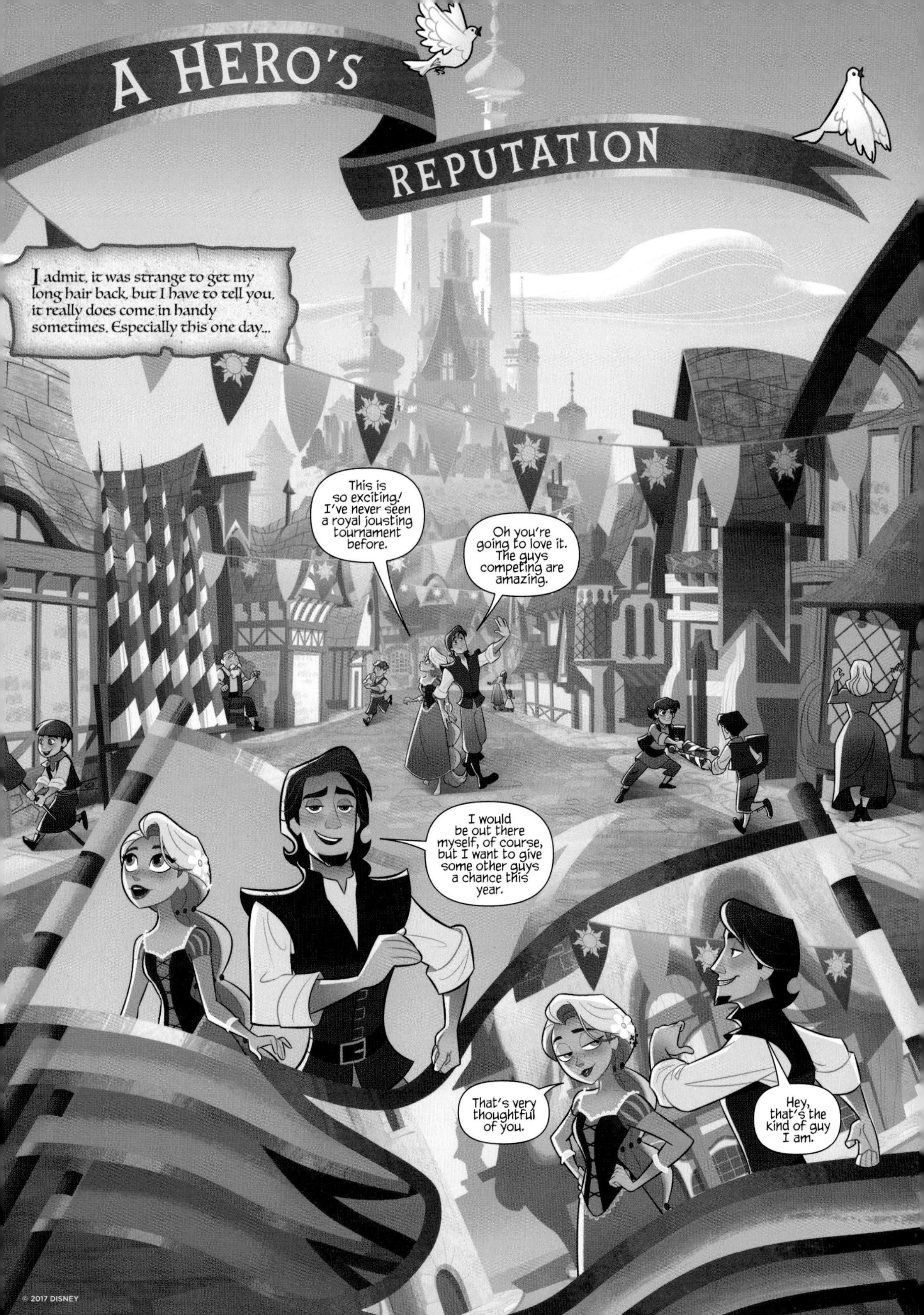
A HERO'S REPUTATION
I admit, it was strange to get my long hair back, but I have to tell you, it really does come in handy sometimes. Especially this one day...
This is so exciting! I've never seen a royal jousting tournament before.
Oh you're going to love it. The guys competing are amazing.
I would be out there myself, of course, but I want to give some other guys a chance this year.
That's very thoughtful of you.
Hey, that's the kind of guy I am.

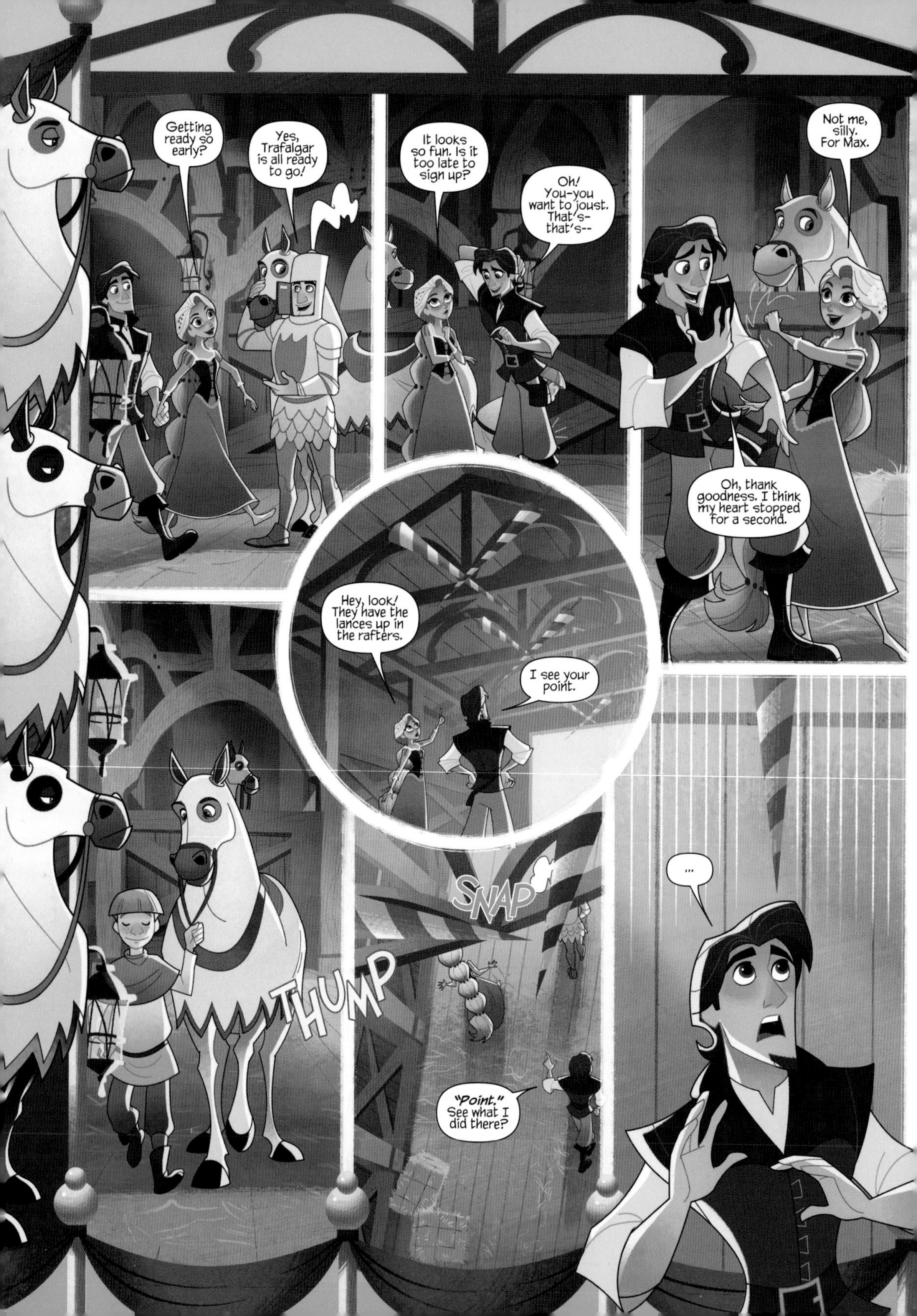

Getting ready so early?
Yes, Trafalgar is all ready to go!
It looks so fun. Is it too late to sign up?
Oh! You-you want to joust. That's- that's--
Not me, silly. For Max.
Oh, thank goodness. I think my heart stopped for a second.
Hey, look! They have the lances up in the rafters.
I see your point.
SNAP
THUMP
"Point." See what I did there?
...

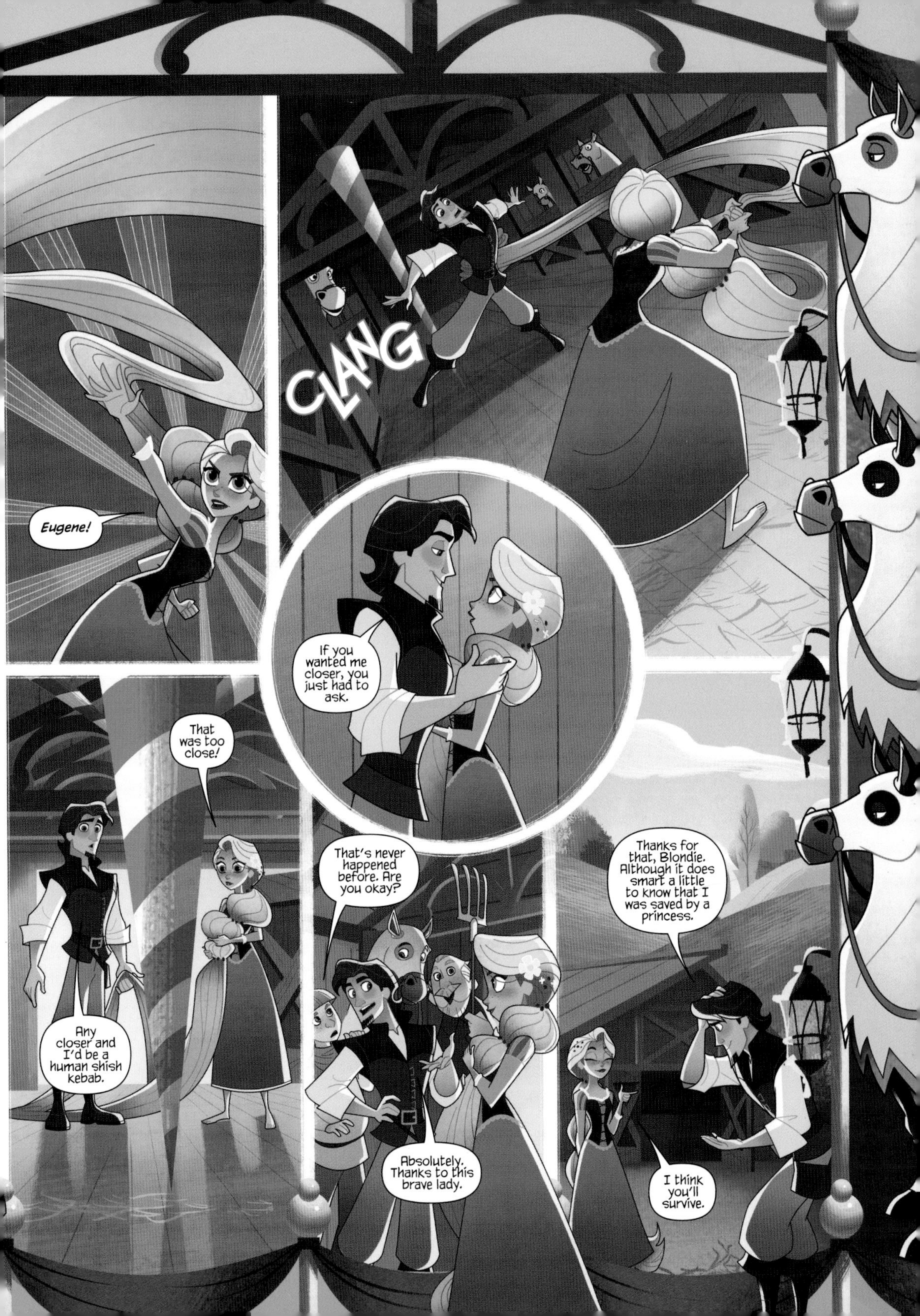
Eugene!
CLANG
If you wanted me closer, you just had to ask.
That was too close!
Any closer and I'd be a human shish kebab.
That's never happened before. Are you okay?
Absolutely. Thanks to this brave lady.
Thanks for that, Blondie. Although it does smart a little to know that I was saved by a princess.
I think you'll survive.

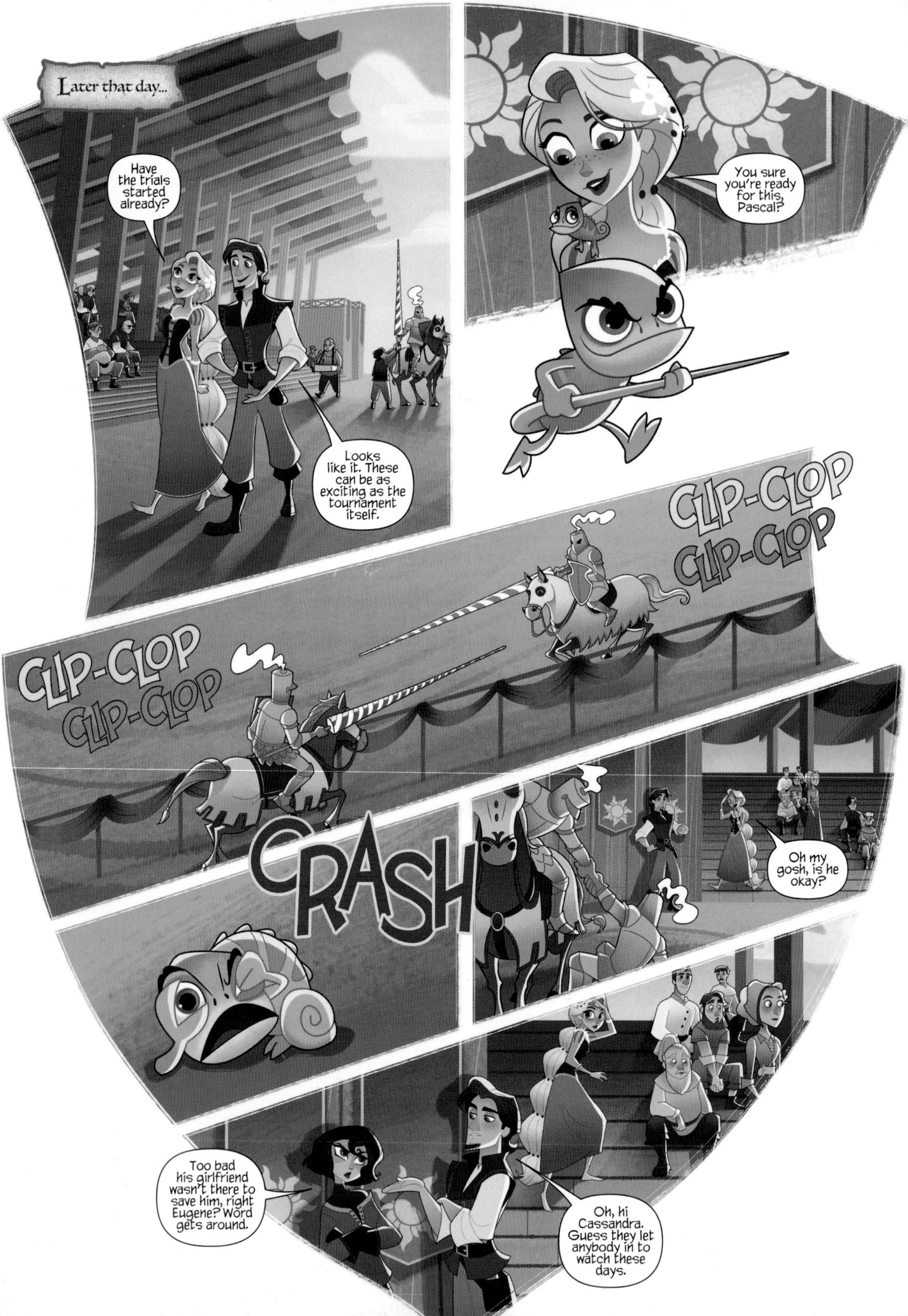
Later that day...
Have the trials started already?
Looks like it. These can be as exciting as the tournament itself.
You sure you're ready for this, Pascal?
CLIP-CLOP
CLIP-CLOP
CLIP-CLOP
CLIP-CLOP
CRASH
Oh my gosh, is he okay?
Too bad his girlfriend wasn't there to save him, right Eugene? Word gets around.
Oh, hi Cassandra. Guess they let anybody in to watch these days.

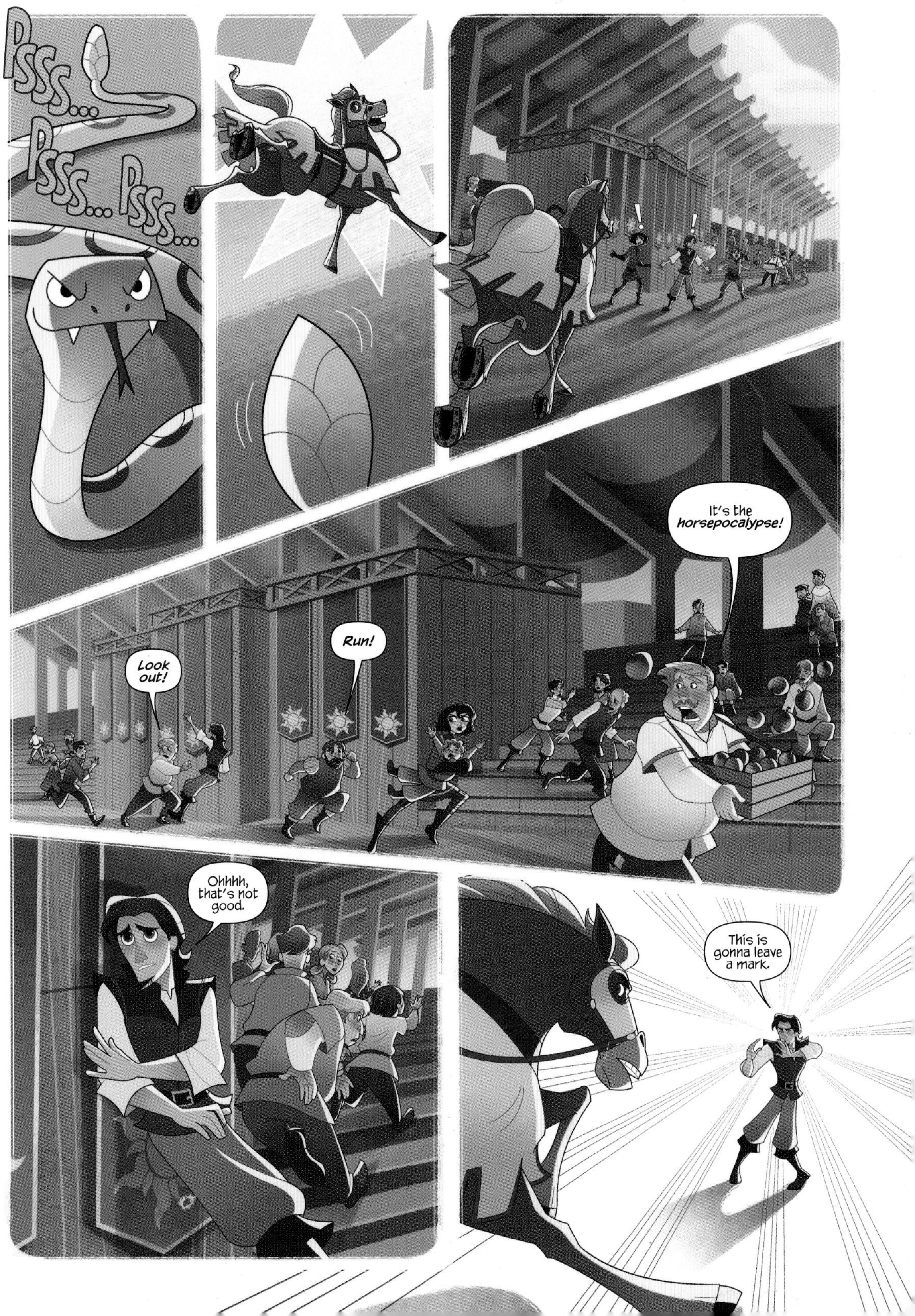
Psss...
Psss... Psss...
It's the horsepocalypse!
Look out!
Run!
Ohhhh, that's not good.
This is gonna leave a mark.

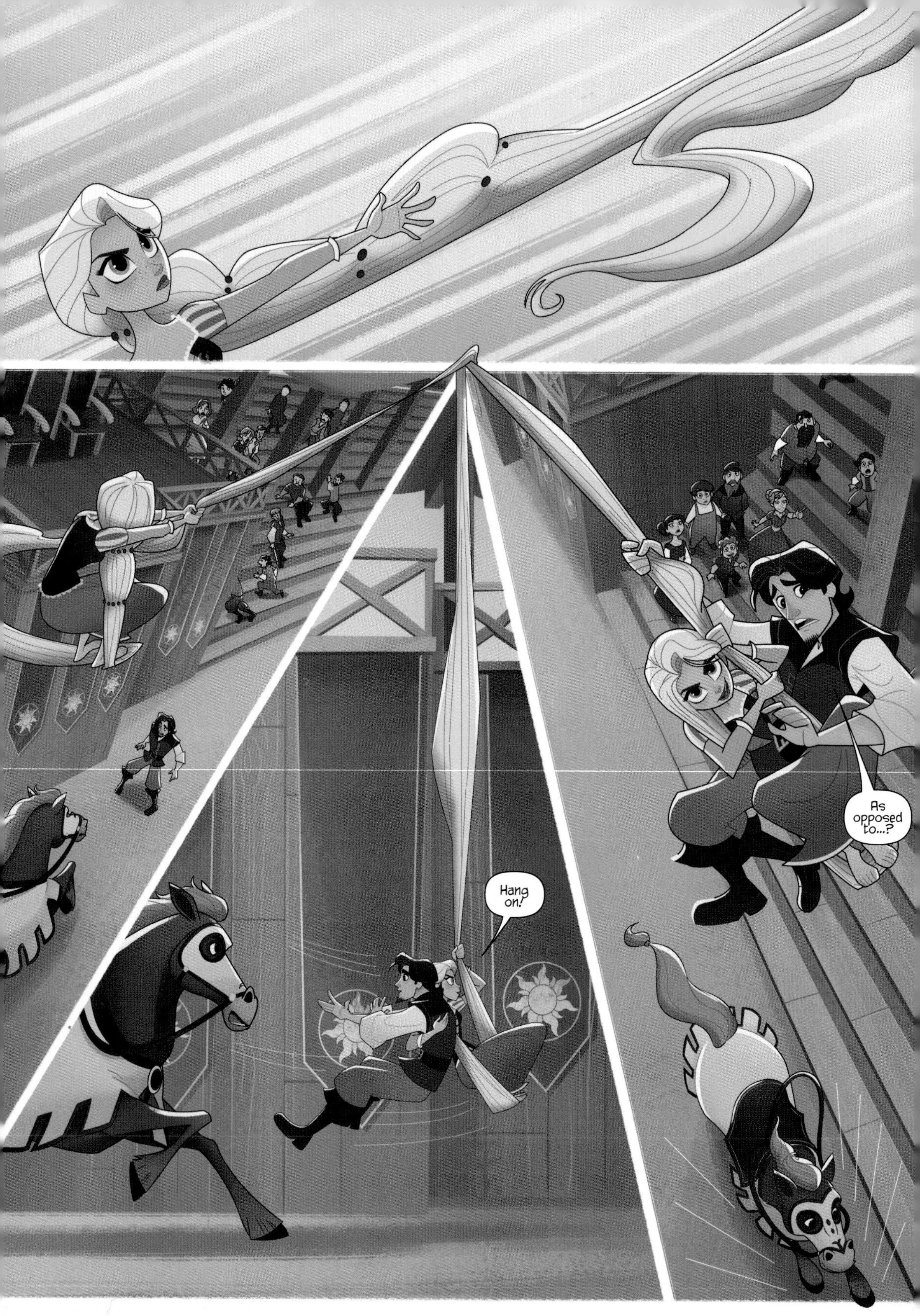
Hang on!
As opposed to...?

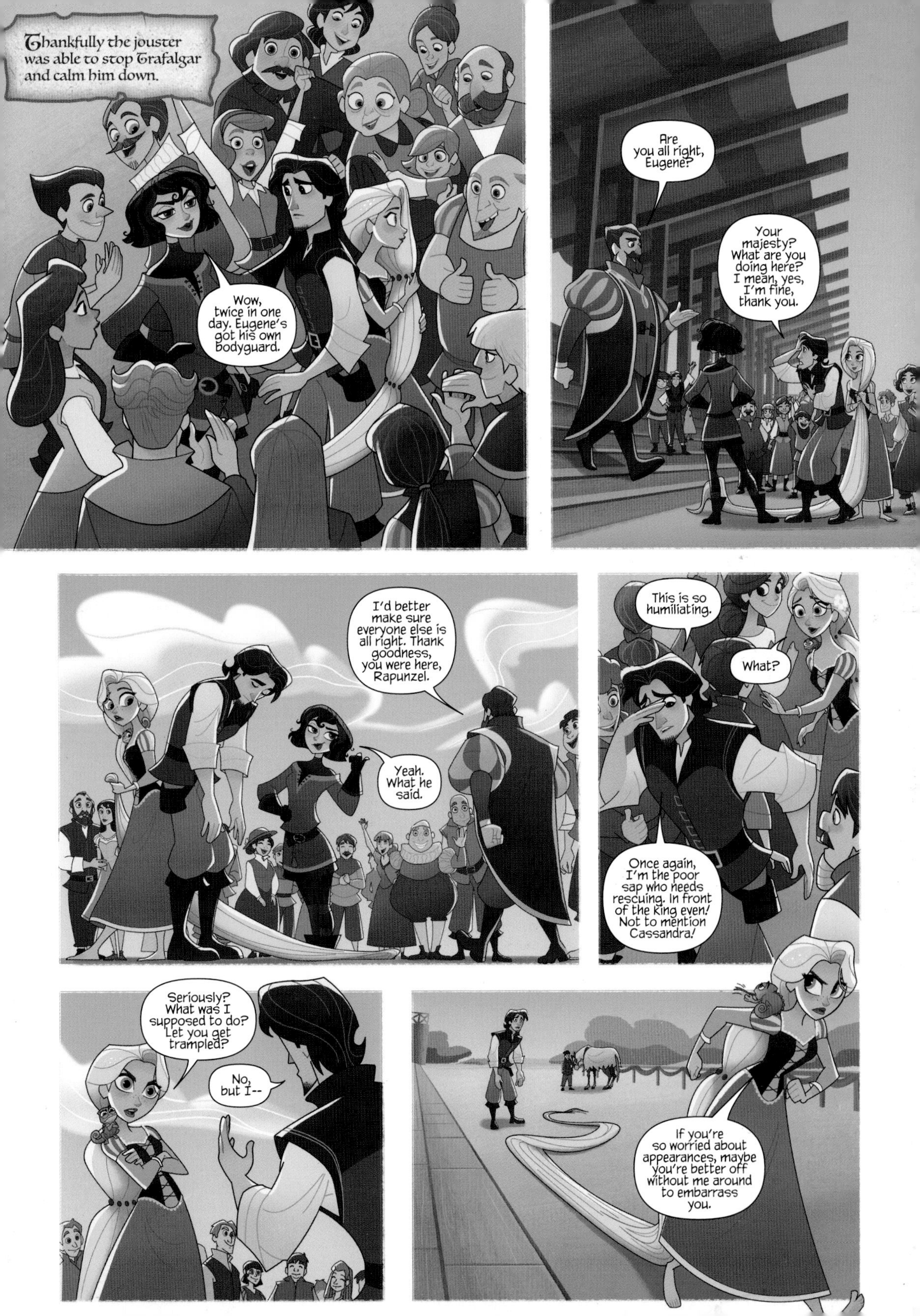
Thankfully the jouster was able to stop Trafalgar and calm him down.
Wow, twice in one day. Eugene's got his own bodyguard.
Are you all right, Eugene?
Your majesty? What are you doing here? I mean, yes, I'm fine, thank you.
I'd better make sure everyone else is all right. Thank goodness, you were here, Rapunzel.
Yeah. What he said.
This is so humiliating.
What?
Once again, I'm the poor sap who needs rescuing. In front of the king even! Not to mention Cassandra!
Seriously? What was I supposed to do? Let you get trampled?
No, but I--
If you're so worried about appearances, maybe you're better off without me around to embarrass you.

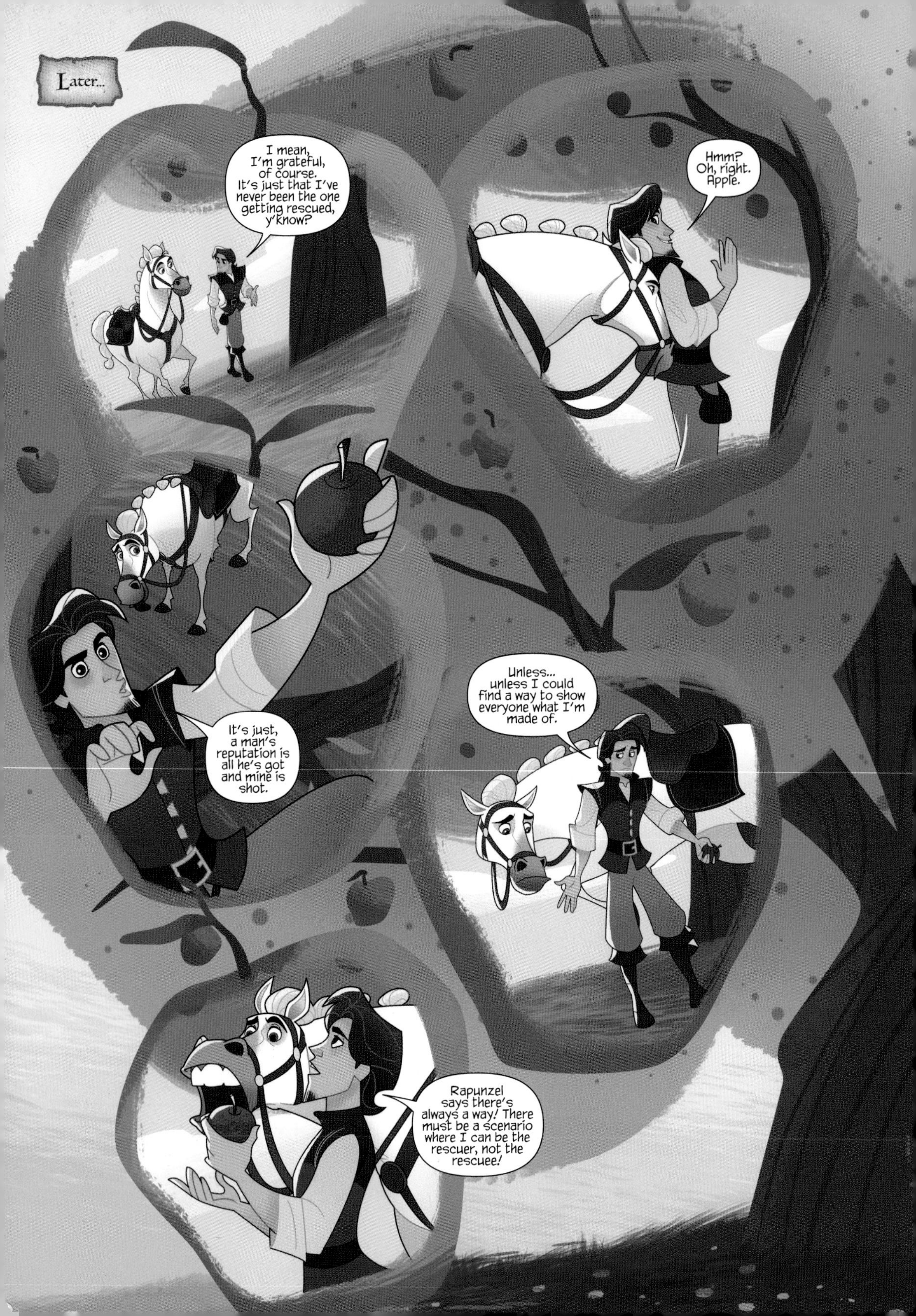
Later...
I mean, I'm grateful, of course. It's just that I've never been the one getting rescued, y'know?
Hmm? Oh, right. Apple.
It's just, a man's reputation is all he's got and mine is shot.
Unless... unless I could find a way to show everyone what I'm made of.
Rapunzel says there's always a way! There must be a scenario where I can be the rescuer, not the rescuee!

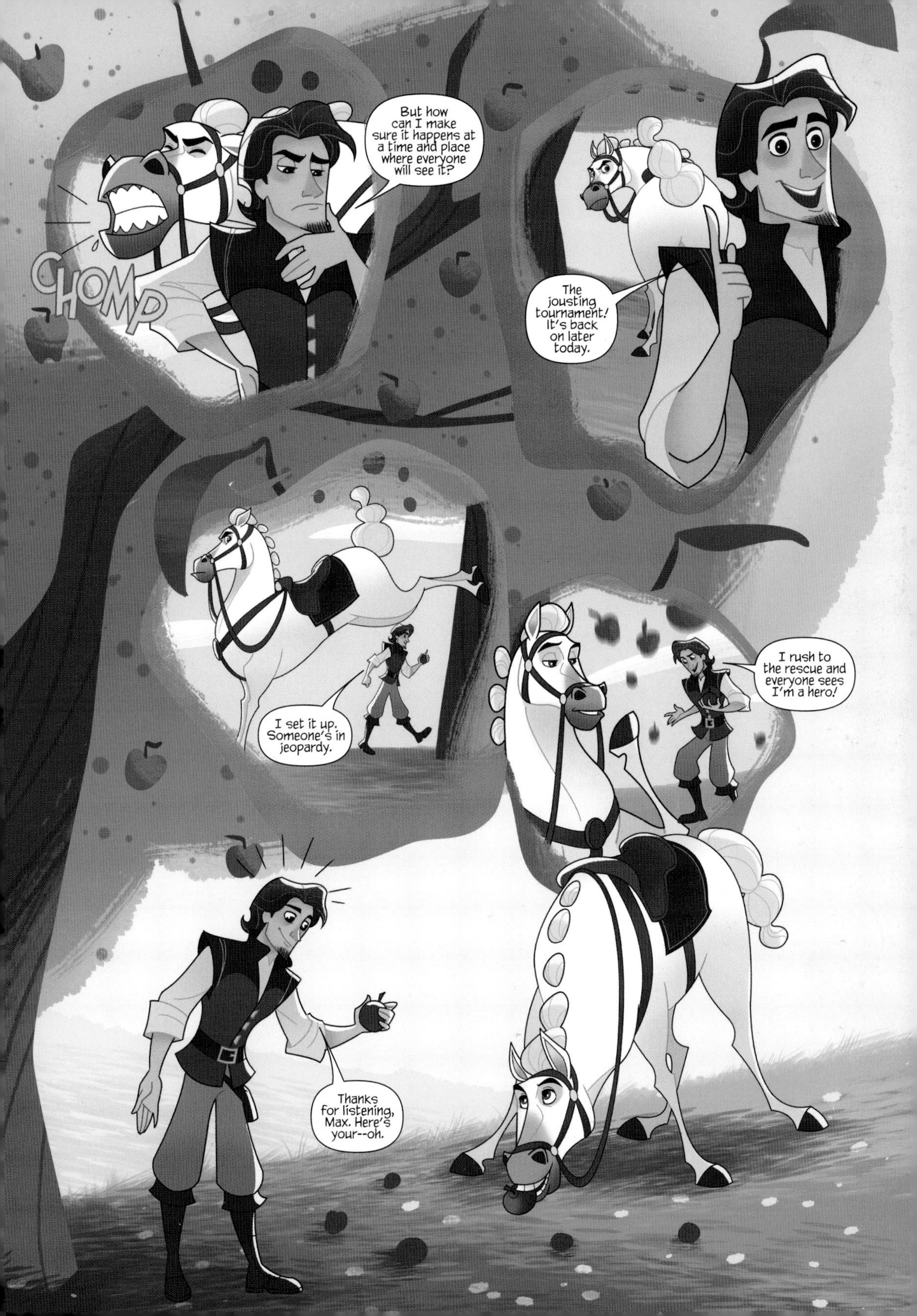
CHOMP
But how can I make sure it happens at a time and place where everyone will see it?
The jousting tournament! It's back on later today.
I set it up. Someone's in jeopardy.
I rush to the rescue and everyone sees I'm a hero!
Thanks for listening, Max. Here's your--oh.

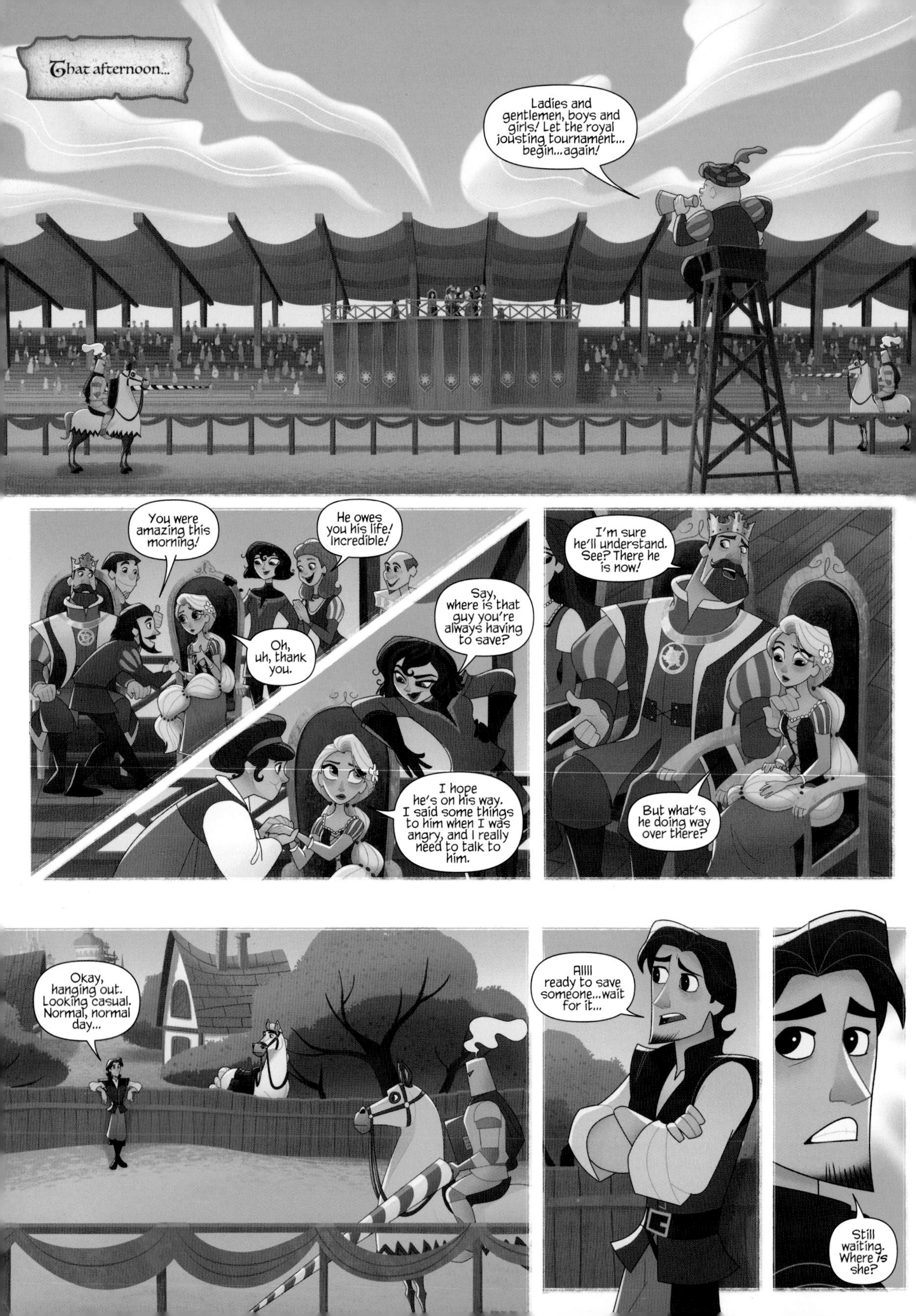
That afternoon...
Ladies and gentlemen, boys and girls! Let the royal jousting tournament... begin...again!
You were amazing this morning!
He owes you his life! Incredible!
Oh, uh, thank you.
Say, where is that guy you're always having to save?
I hope he's on his way. I said some things to him when I was angry, and I really need to talk to him.
I'm sure he'll understand. See? There he is now!
But what's he doing way over there?
Okay, hanging out. Looking casual. Normal, normal day...
Allll ready to save someone...wait for it...
Still waiting. Where is she?

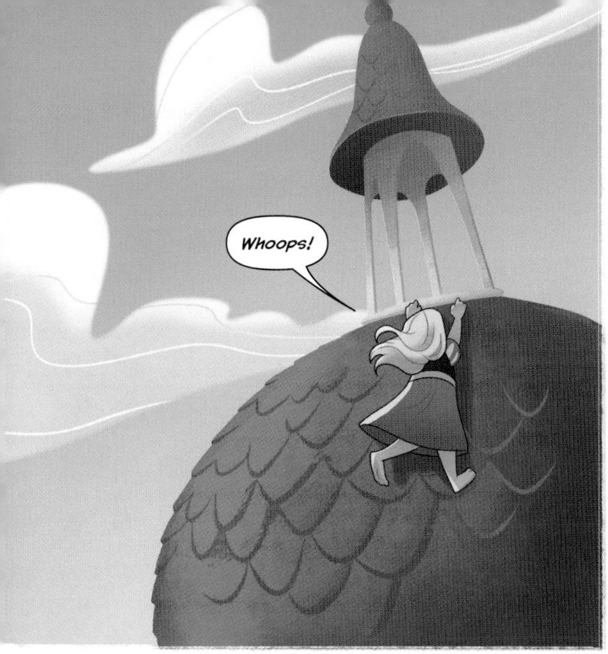
Whoops!

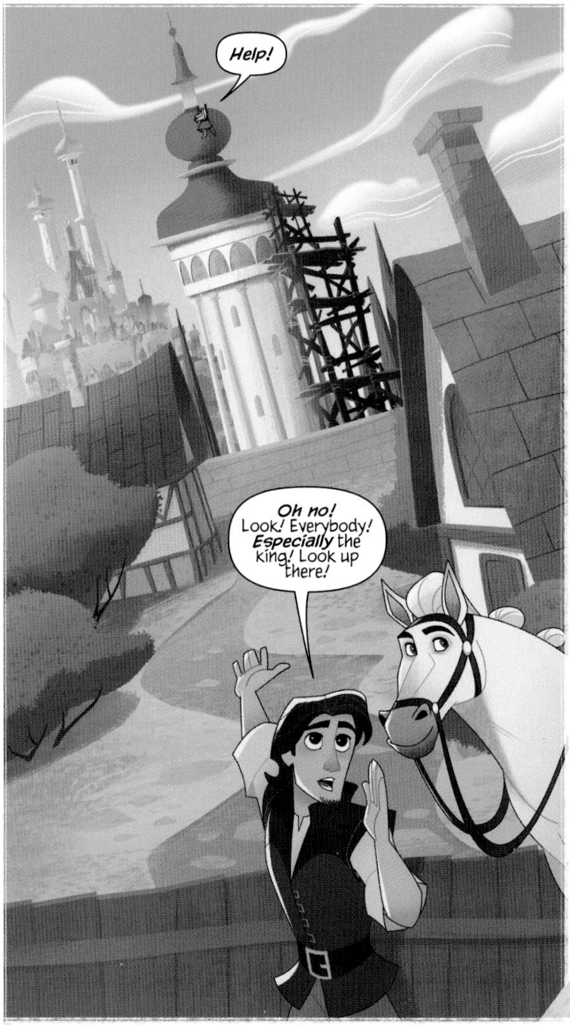
Help!
Oh no! Look! Everybody! ***Especially*** the king! Look up there!

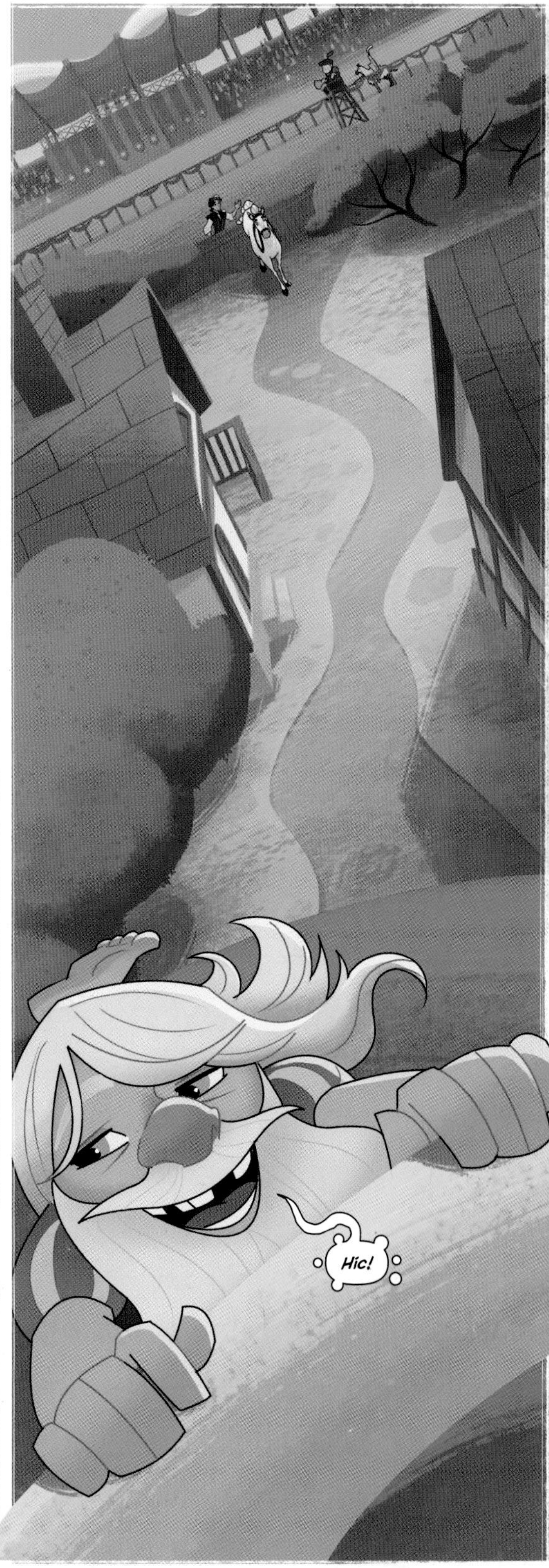
Hic!

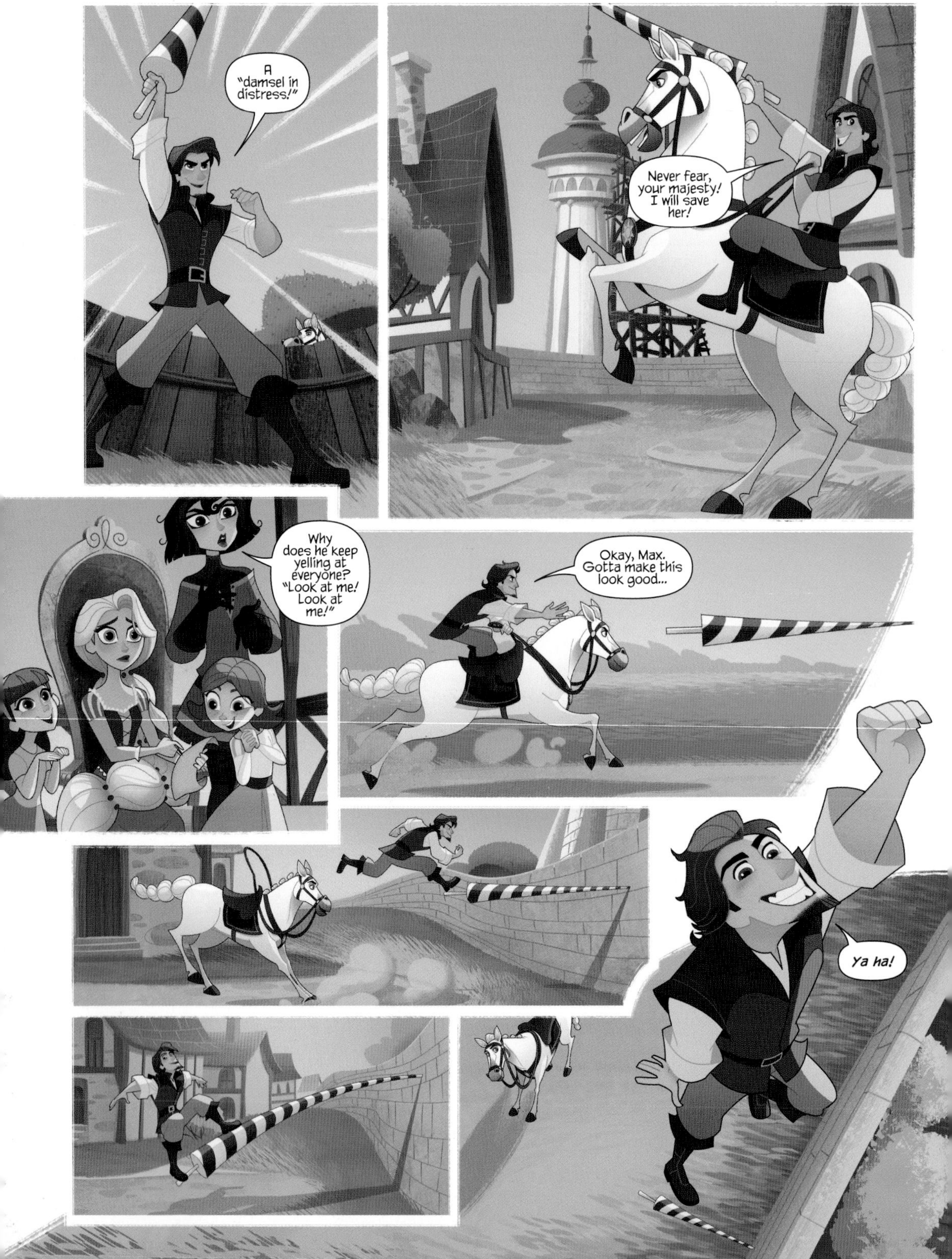
A "damsel in distress!"
Never fear, your majesty! I will save her!
Why does he keep yelling at everyone? "Look at me! Look at me!"
Okay, Max. Gotta make this look good...
Ya ha!

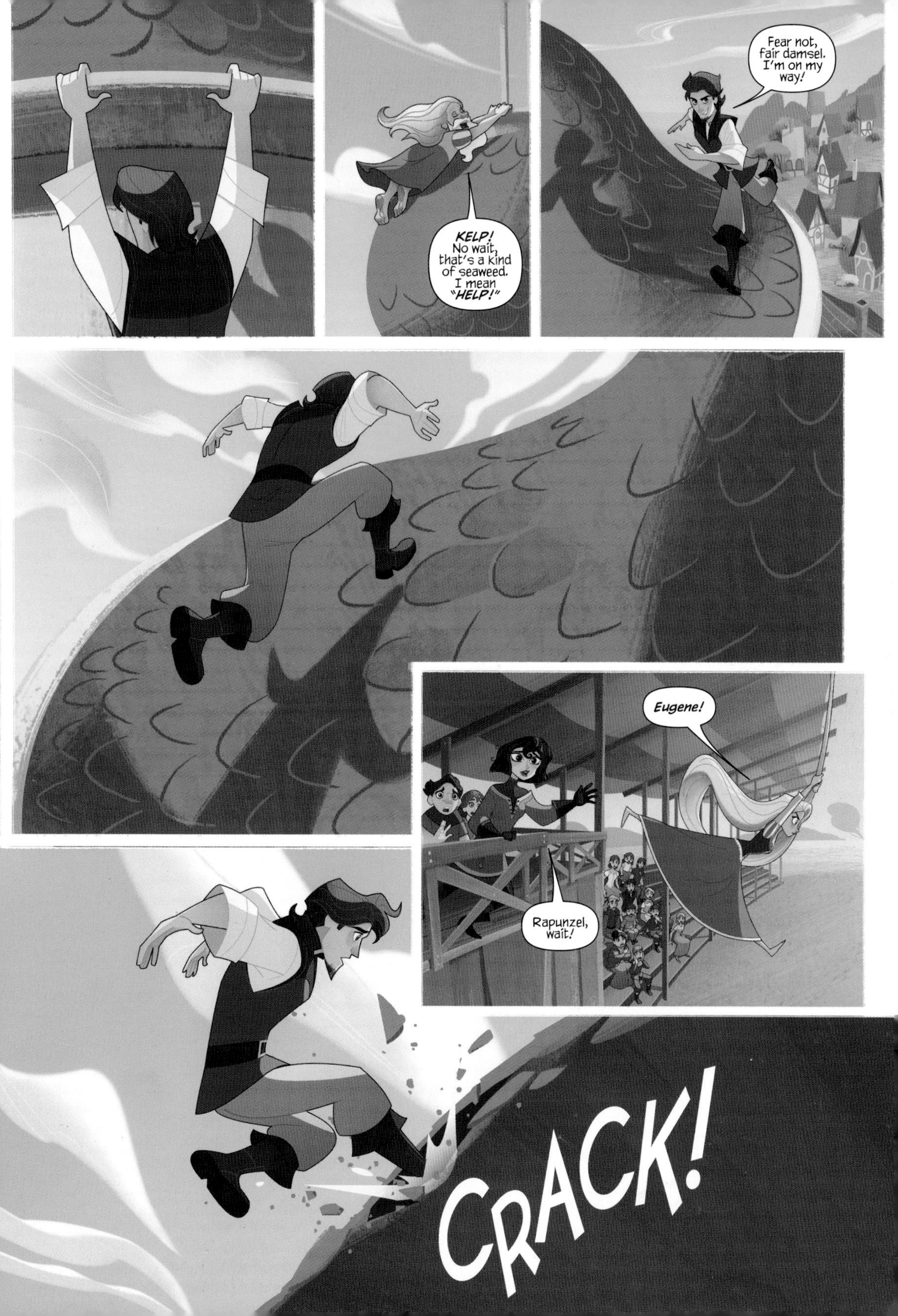
KELP! No wait, that's a kind of seaweed. I mean "HELP!"
Fear not, fair damsel. I'm on my way!
Eugene!
Rapunzel, wait!
CRACK!

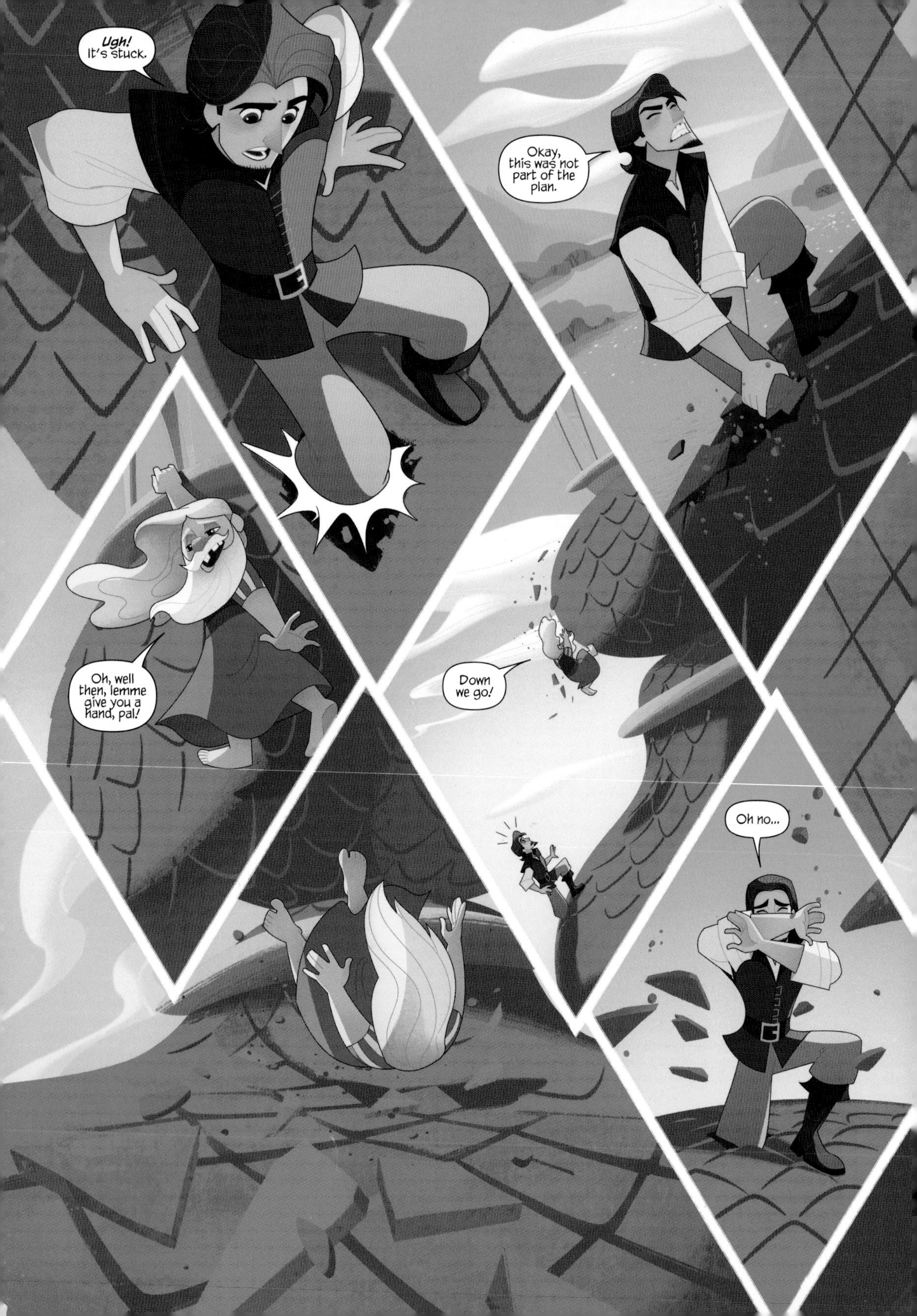

Ugh! It's stuck.
Okay, this was not part of the plan.
Oh, well then, lemme give you a hand, pal!
Down we go!
Oh no...

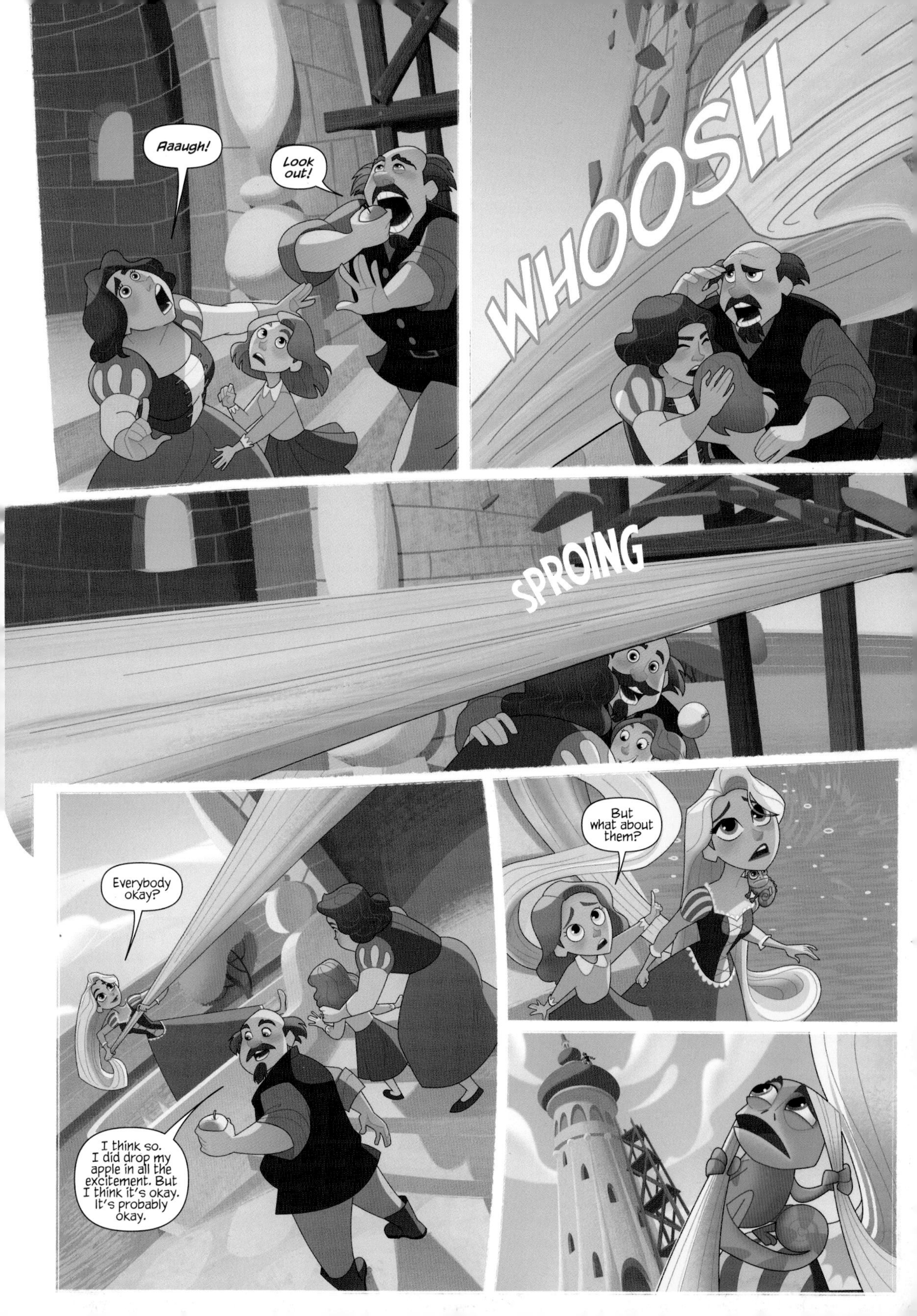
Aaaugh!
Look out!
WHOOSH
SPROING
Everybody okay?
I think so. I did drop my apple in all the excitement. But I think it's okay. It's probably okay.
But what about them?

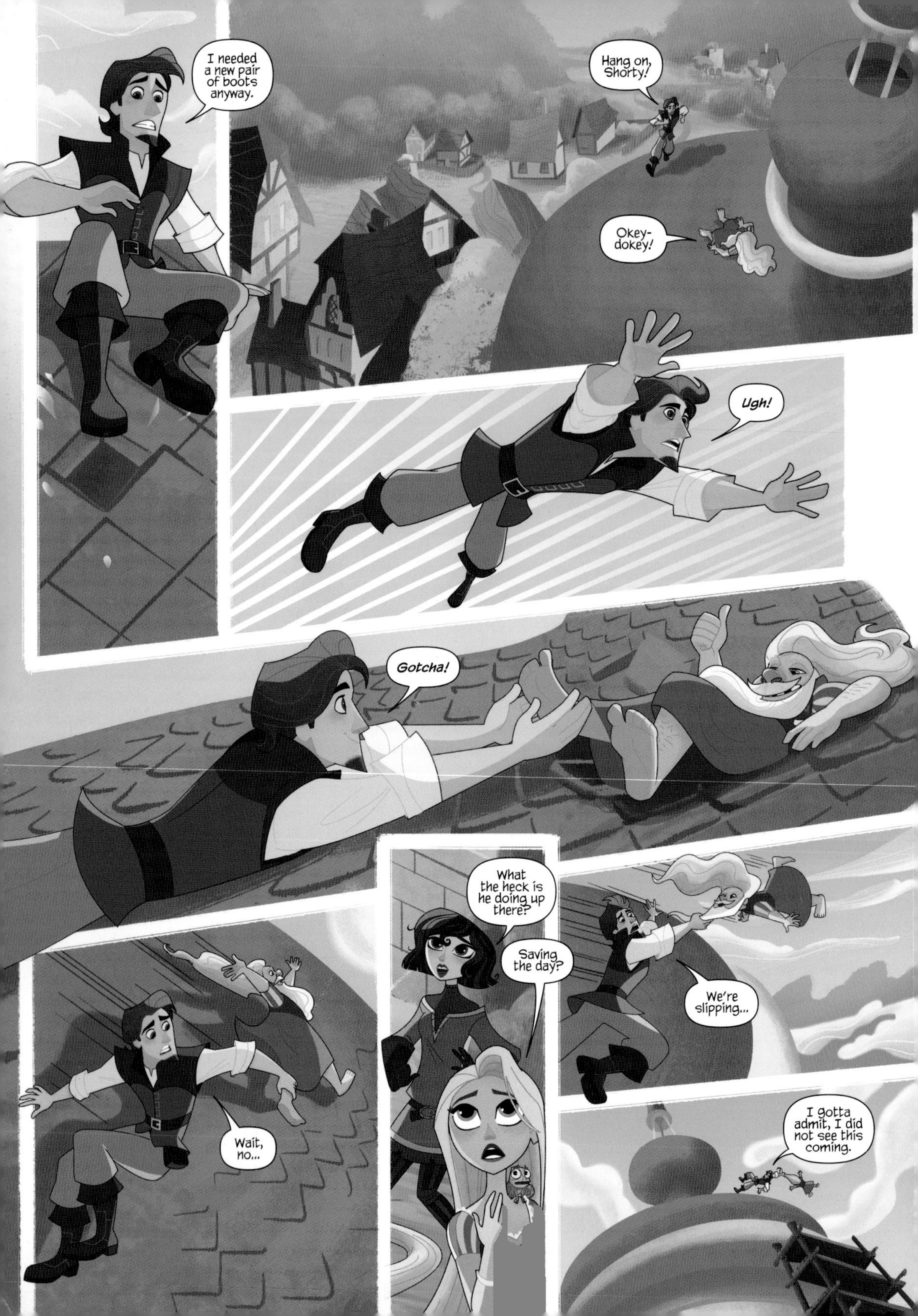
I needed a new pair of boots anyway.
Hang on, Shorty!
Okey-dokey!
Ugh!
Gotcha!
Wait, no...
What the heck is he doing up there?
Saving the day?
We're slipping...
I gotta admit, I did not see this coming.

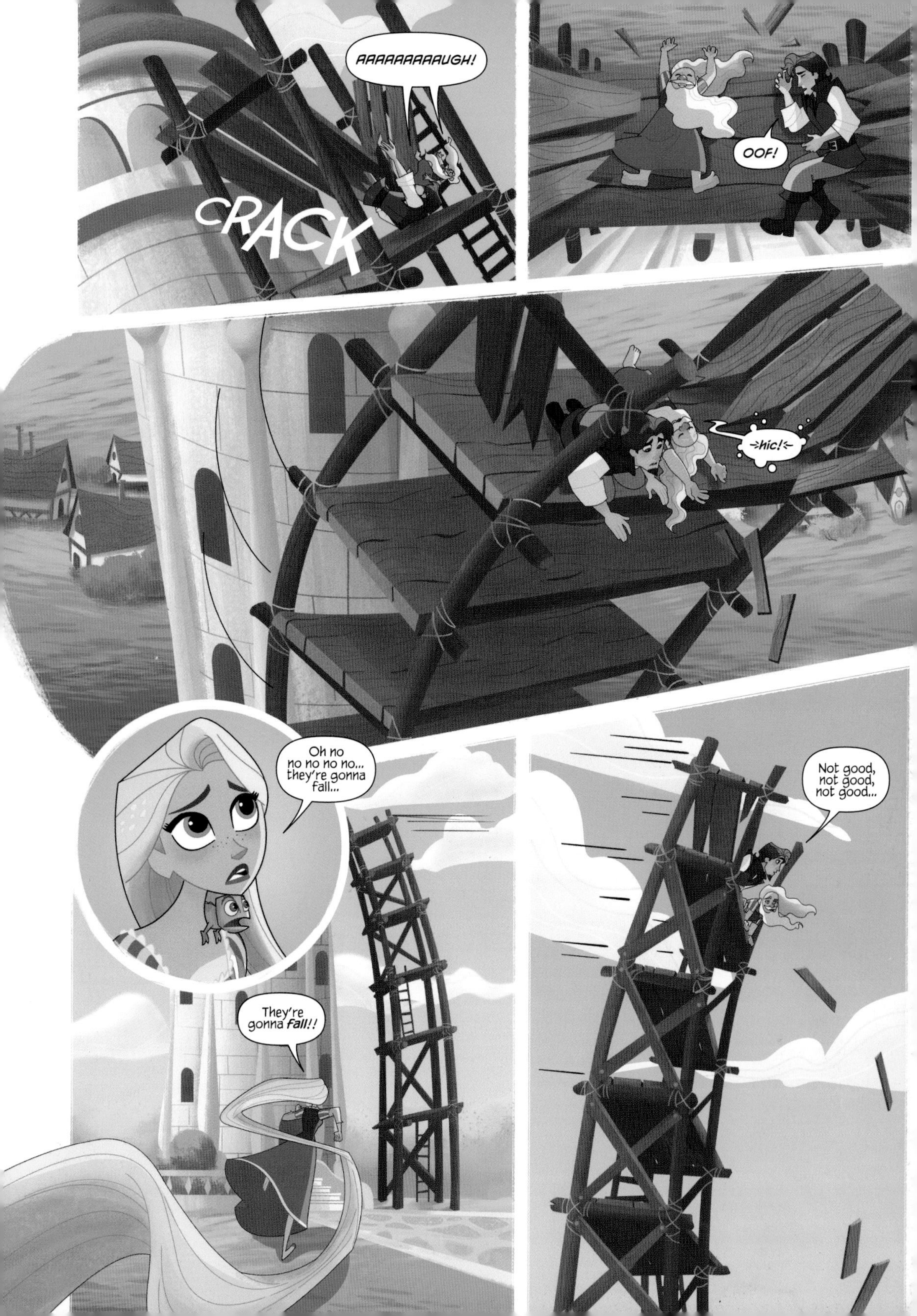
AAAAAAAAAUGH!
CRACK
OOF!
~hic!~
Oh no no no no no... they're gonna fall...
They're gonna **fall**!!
Not good, not good, not good...

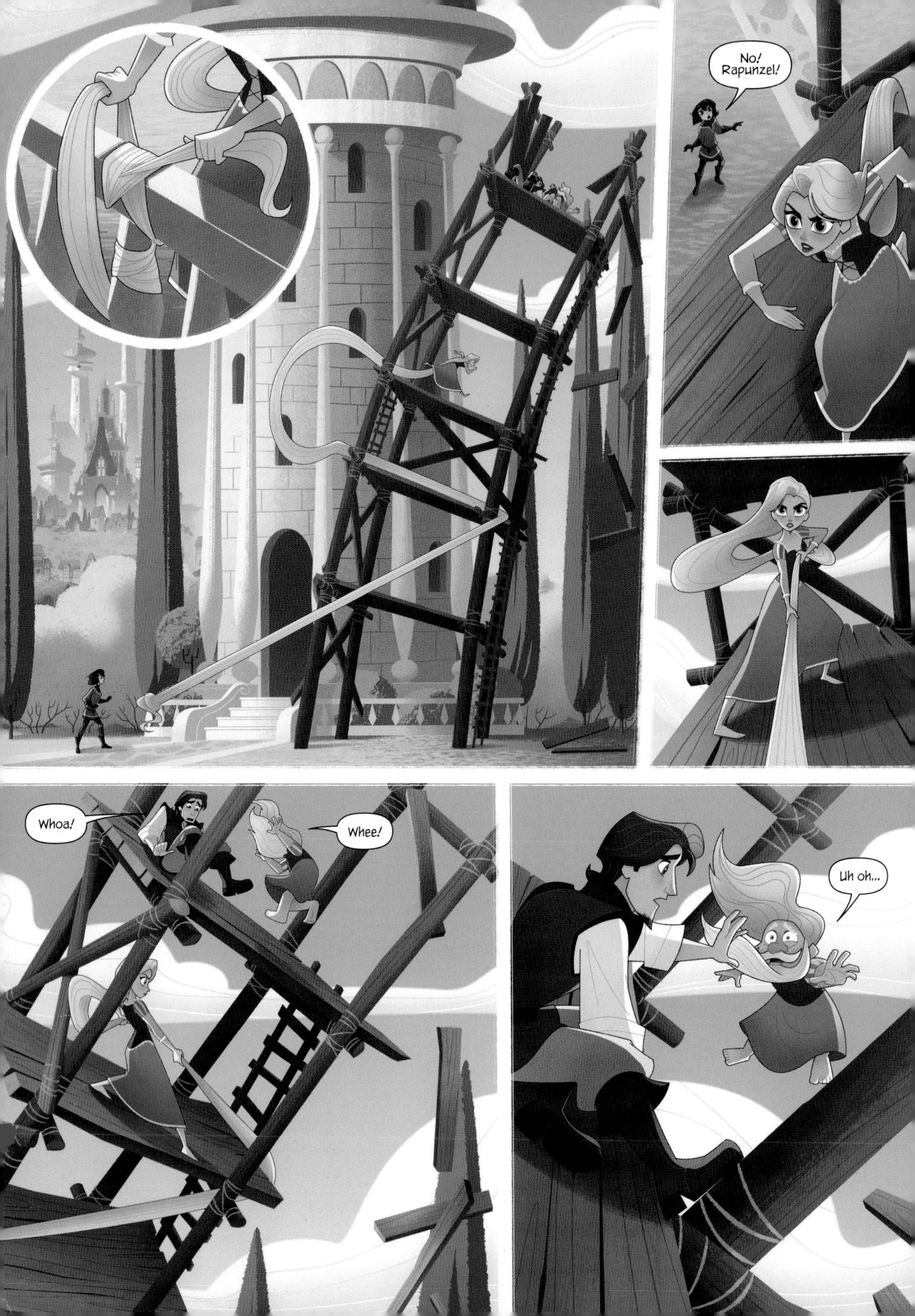
No! Rapunzel!
Whoa!
Whee!
Uh oh...

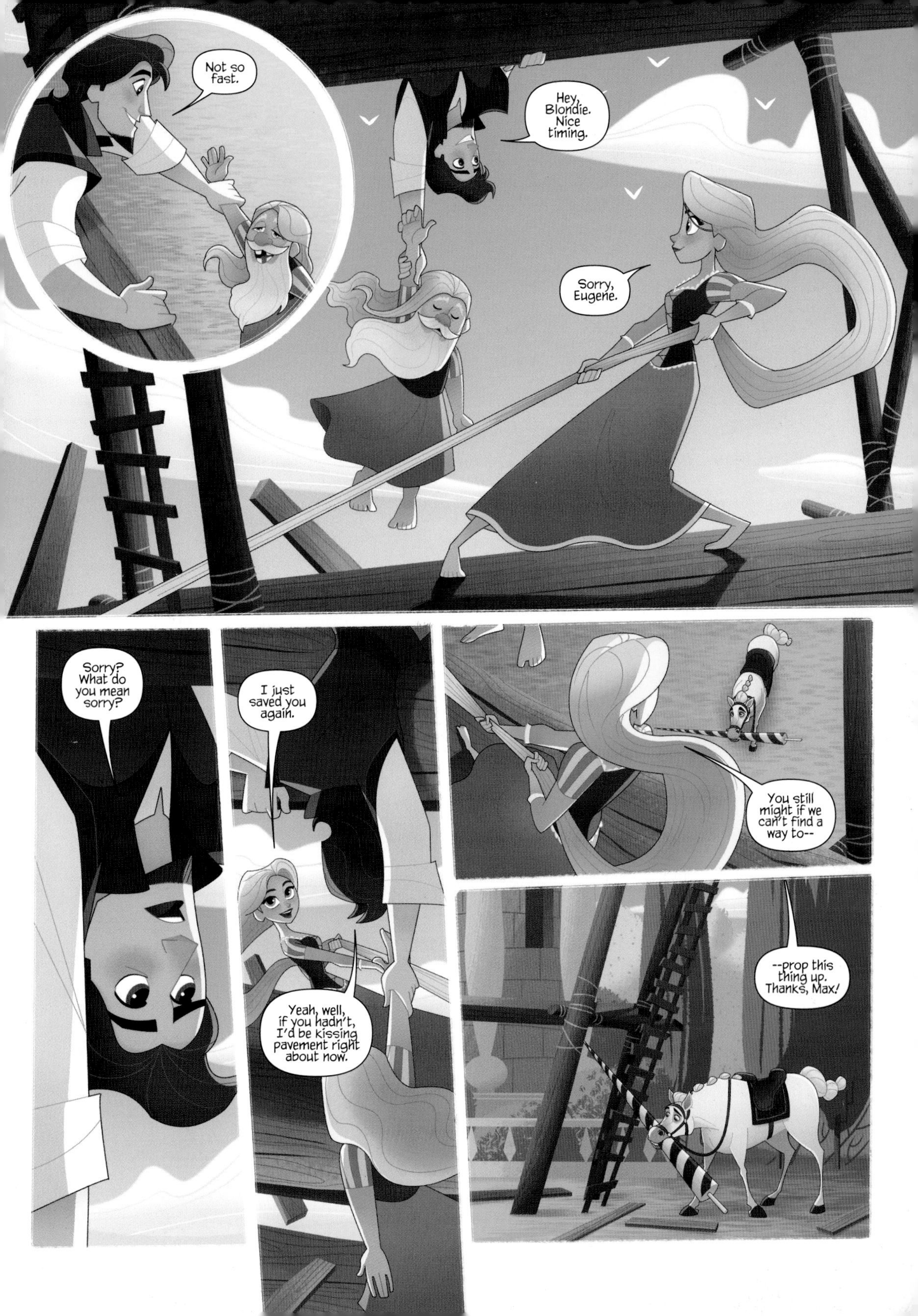

Not so fast.
Hey, Blondie. Nice timing.
Sorry, Eugene.
Sorry? What do you mean sorry?
I just saved you again.
Yeah, well, if you hadn't, I'd be kissing pavement right about now.
You still might if we can't find a way to--
--prop this thing up. Thanks, Max!

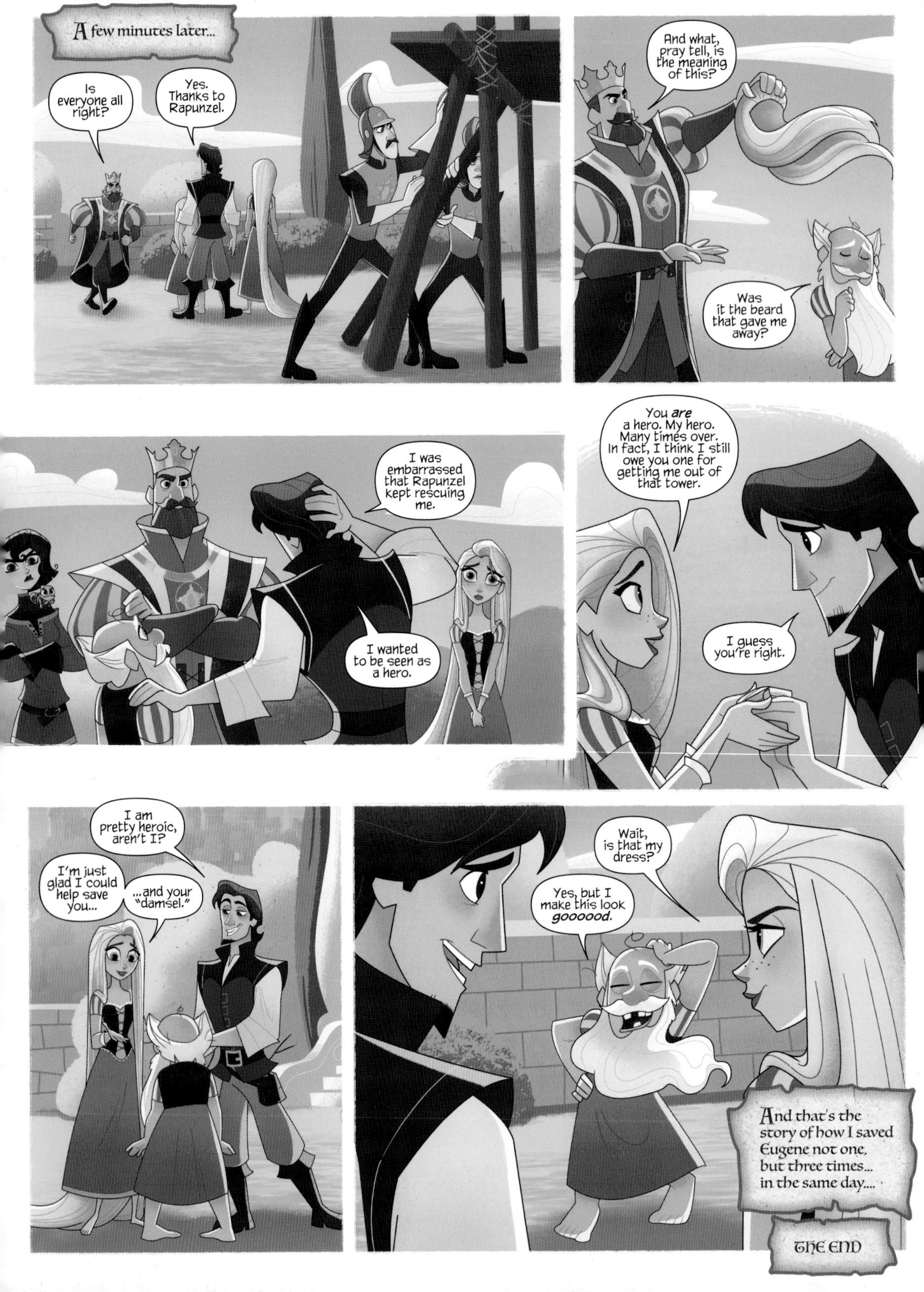
A few minutes later...
Is everyone all right?
Yes. Thanks to Rapunzel.
And what, pray tell, is the meaning of this?
Was it the beard that gave me away?
I was embarrassed that Rapunzel kept rescuing me.
I wanted to be seen as a hero.
You *are* a hero. My hero. Many times over. In fact, I think I still owe you one for getting me out of that tower.
I guess you're right.
I am pretty heroic, aren't I?
I'm just glad I could help save you...
...and your "damsel."
Wait, is that my dress?
Yes, but I make this look *goooood*.
And that's the story of how I saved Eugene not one, but three times... in the same day....
THE END

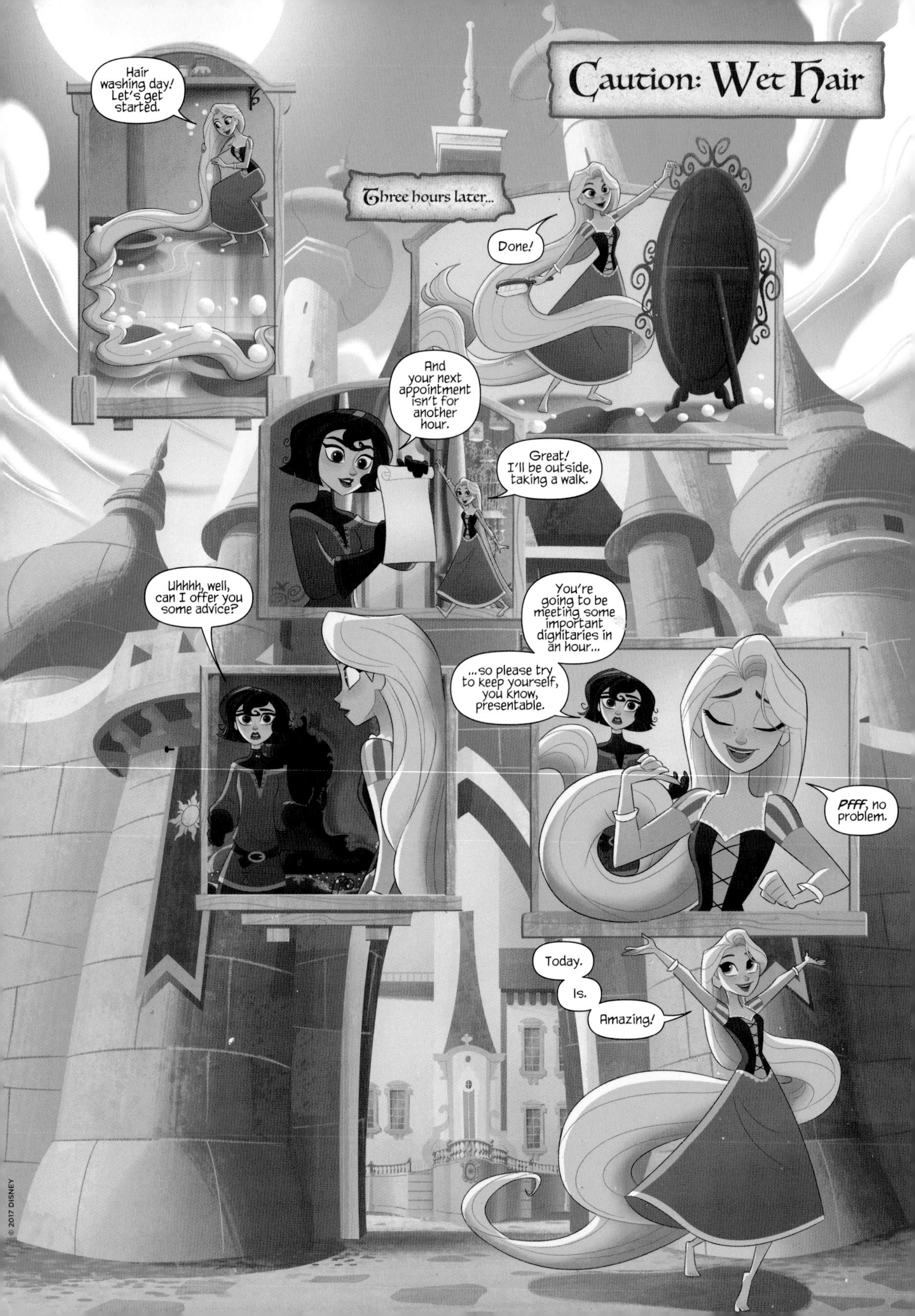
Caution: Wet Hair
Hair washing day! Let's get started.
Three hours later...
Done!
And your next appointment isn't for another hour.
Great! I'll be outside, taking a walk.
Uhhhh, well, can I offer you some advice?
You're going to be meeting some important dignitaries in an hour...
...so please try to keep yourself, you know, presentable.
PFFF, no problem.
Today.
Is.
Amazing!
© 2017 DISNEY

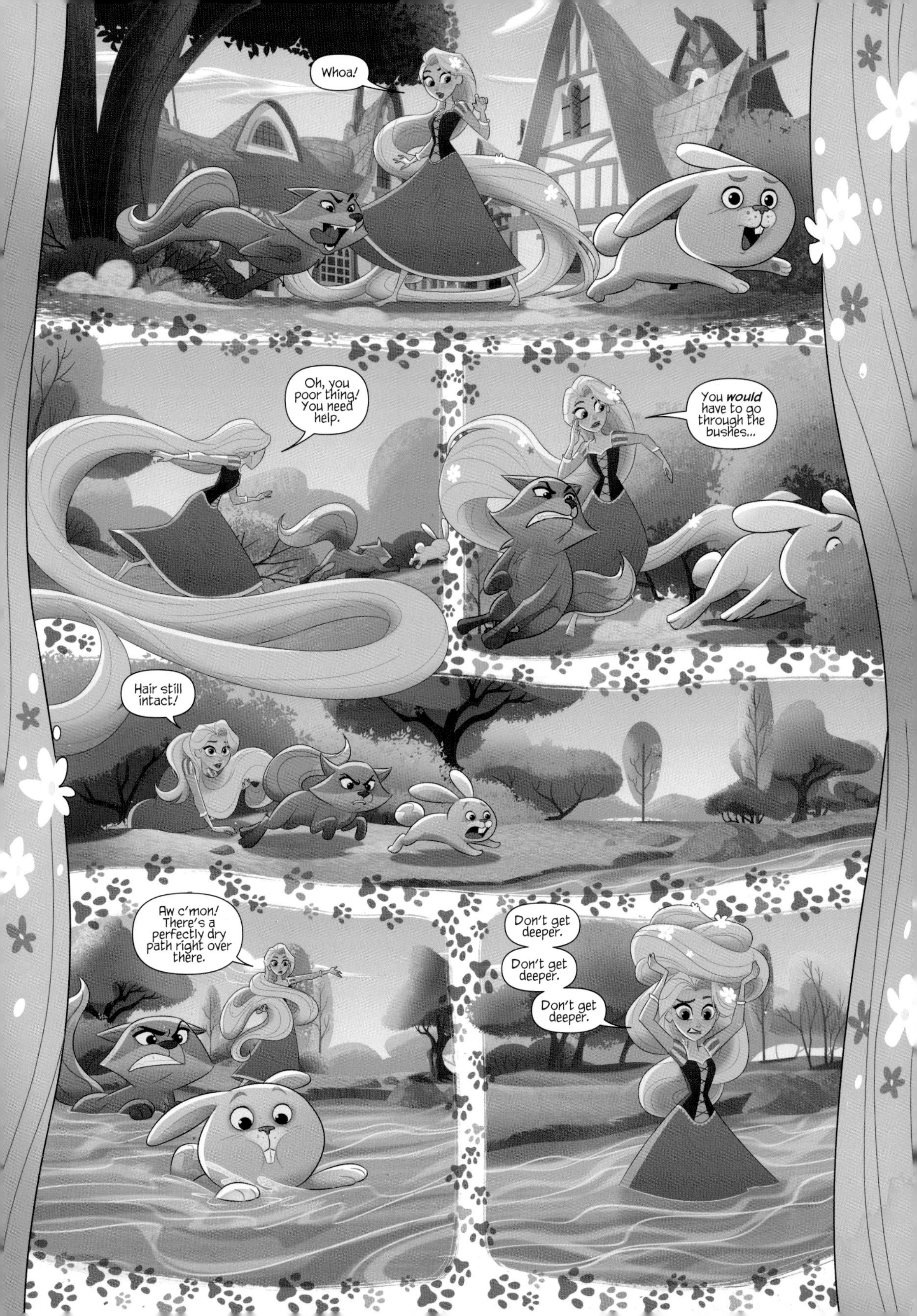
Whoa!
Oh, you poor thing! You need help.
You *would* have to go through the bushes...
Hair still intact!
Aw c'mon! There's a perfectly dry path right over there.
Don't get deeper.
Don't get deeper.
Don't get deeper.

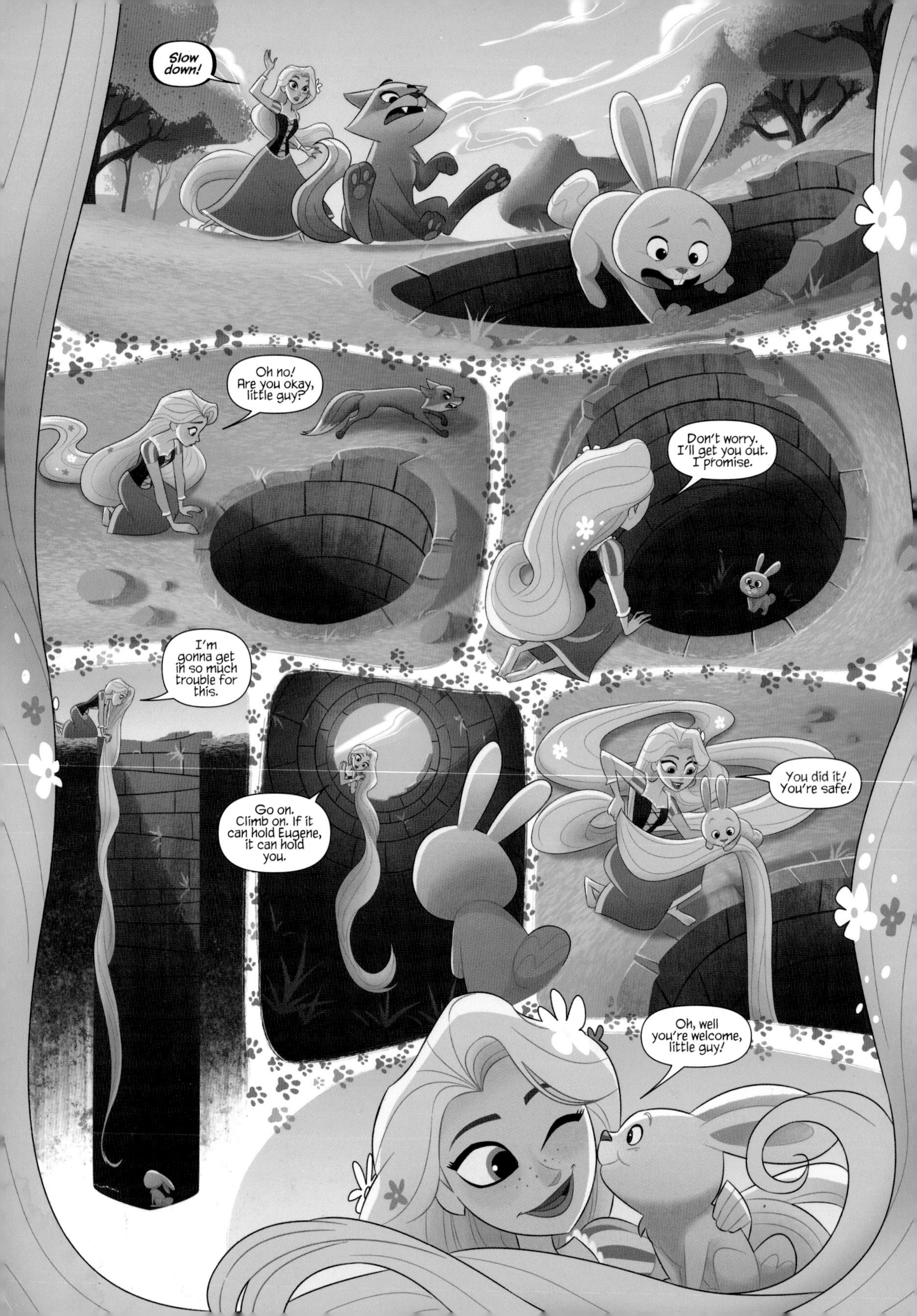
Slow down!
Oh no! Are you okay, little guy?
Don't worry. I'll get you out. I promise.
I'm gonna get in so much trouble for this.
Go on. Climb on. If it can hold Eugene, it can hold you.
You did it! You're safe!
Oh, well you're welcome, little guy!

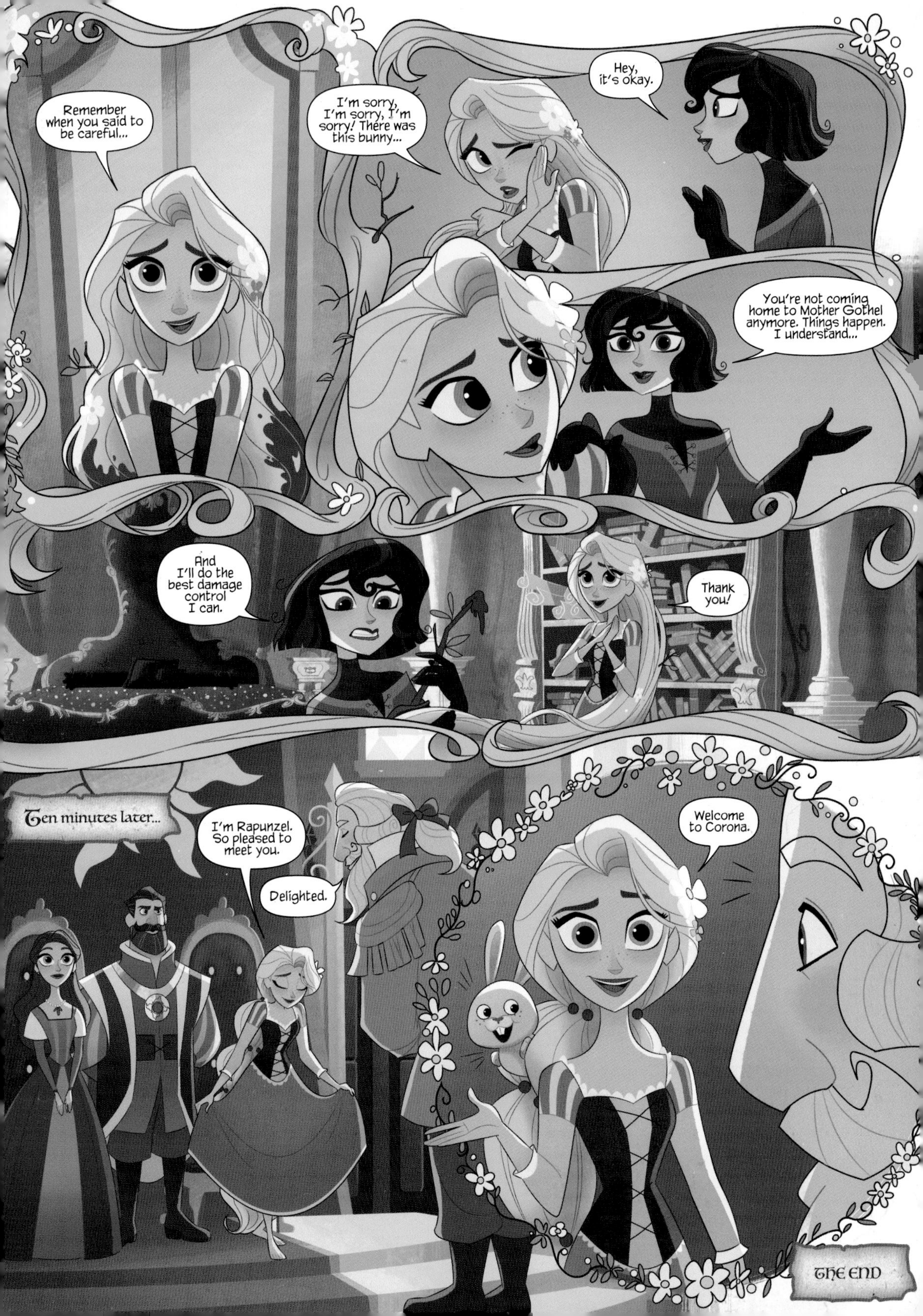

Remember when you said to be careful...
I'm sorry, I'm sorry, I'm sorry! There was this bunny...
Hey, it's okay.
You're not coming home to Mother Gothel anymore. Things happen. I understand...
And I'll do the best damage control I can.
Thank you!
Ten minutes later...
I'm Rapunzel. So pleased to meet you.
Delighted.
Welcome to Corona.
THE END

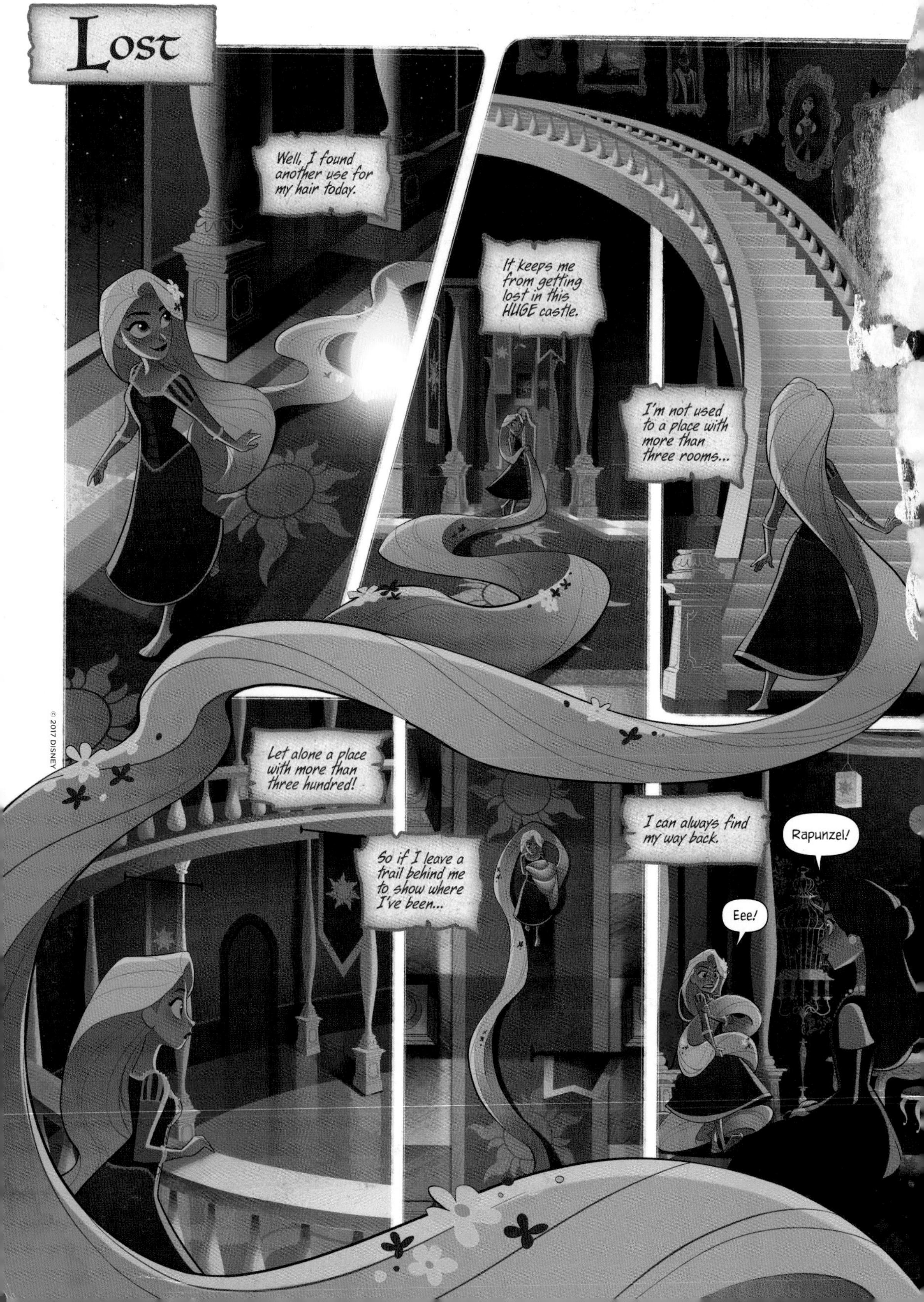
Lost
Well, I found another use for my hair today.
It keeps me from getting lost in this HUGE castle.
I'm not used to a place with more than three rooms...
Let alone a place with more than three hundred!
So if I leave a trail behind me to show where I've been...
I can always find my way back.
Rapunzel!
Eee!

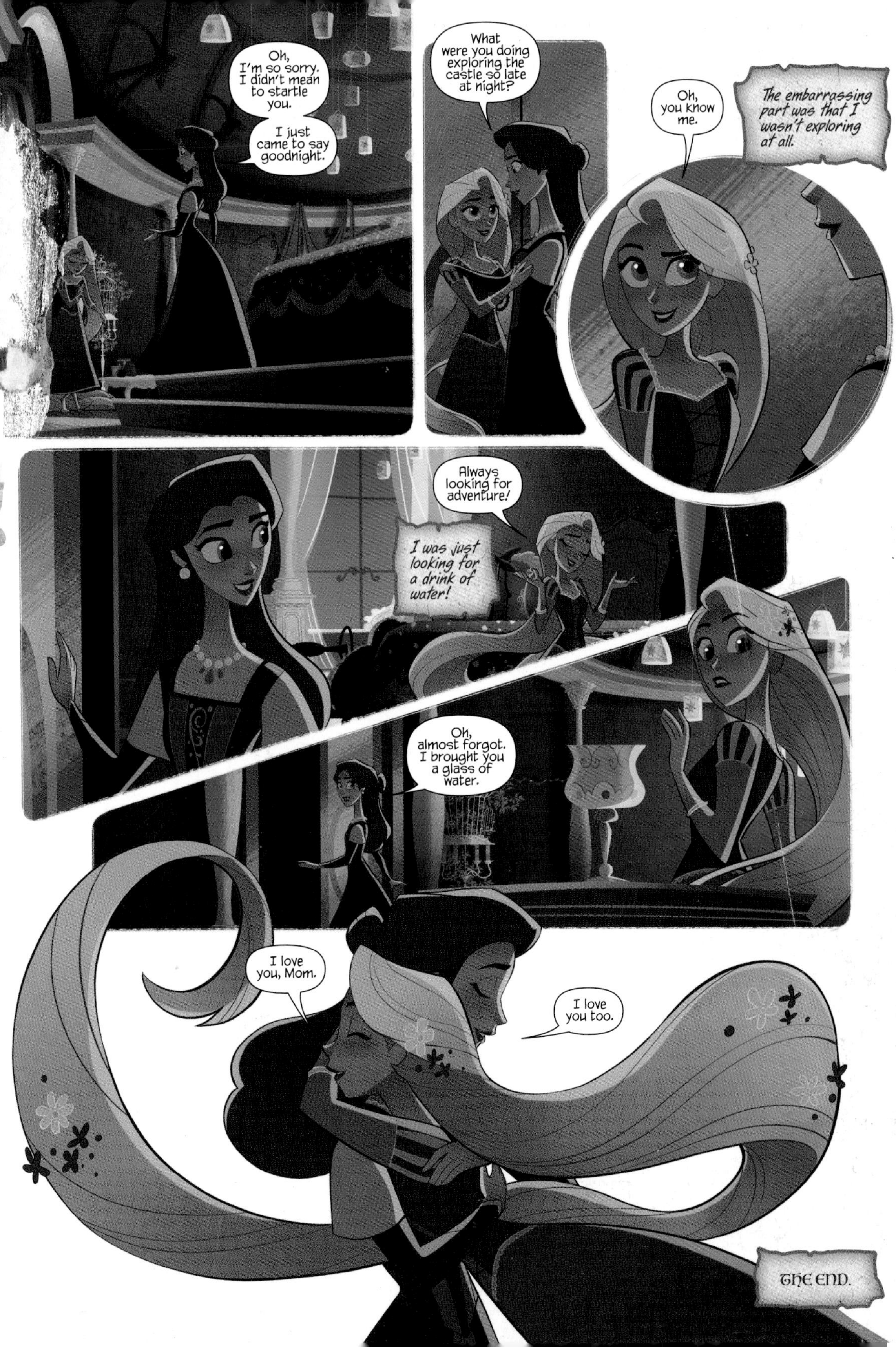

Oh, I'm so sorry. I didn't mean to startle you.
I just came to say goodnight.
What were you doing exploring the castle so late at night?
Oh, you know me.
The embarrassing part was that I wasn't exploring at all.
Always looking for adventure!
I was just looking for a drink of water!
Oh, almost forgot. I brought you a glass of water.
I love you, Mom.
I love you too.
THE END.

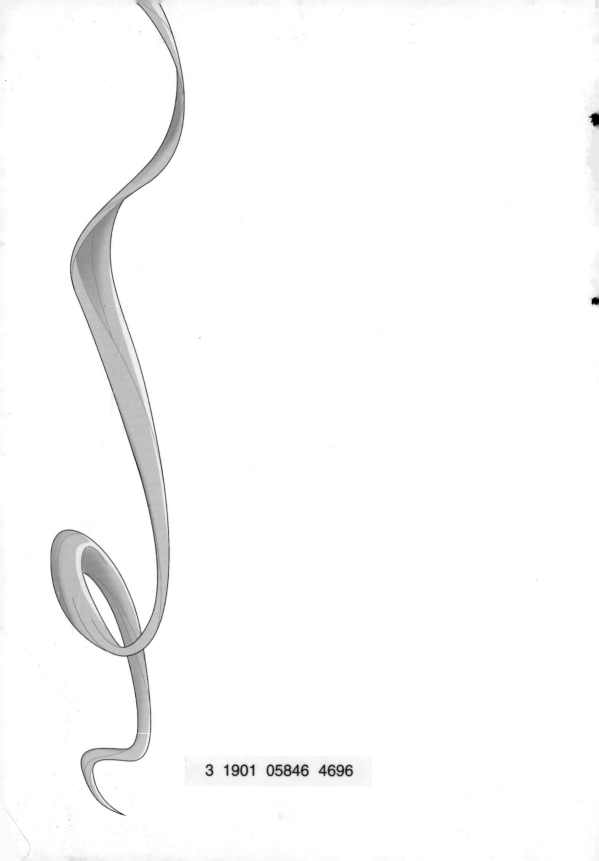